FEVER TREE

Tim Applegate
Amberjack Publishing
New York, New York

Amberjack Publishing
228 Park Avenue S #89611
New York, NY 10003-1502
http://amberjackpublishing.com

Publisher's Cataloging-in-Publication data

Names: Applegate, Tim, author.
Title: Fever Tree / by Tim Applegate.
Identifiers: ISBN 9780997237733 (pbk.) | 9780997237740 (ebook) | LCCN 2016930498.
Description: New York [New York] : Amberjack Publishing, 2016.
Subjects: LCSH Florida—Fiction. | Drugs—Fiction. | Writers—Fiction. | Criminals—Fiction.| BISAC FICTION / General.
Classification: LCC PS3601.P664 F48 2016 | DDC 813.6 –dc23

Cover Design: Red Couch Creative, Inc.
Artwork: Marco Smouse

Printed in the United States of America

"There are always two plots:
a man rides into town, or a man leaves."
Penelope Scambly Schott
Sometimes I Sleep in Dufur

ONE

1

That afternoon he crossed over the last mountain pass and dropped down into the valley, into hardwood forest, hardwood swamp. Hill country for the next twenty miles but bottomland too, brackish water the color of iced tea swirling around trunks of cypress, the swamp's oldest trees. Slowing down, taking his time, avoiding the interstate for less-traveled roads to satisfy an urge, an ache, for real country, for red clay. Not a watery bowl of grits at some shiny new franchise off Exit 36 but an honest-to-God barbeque joint owned by the granddaughter of the man who first opened it, the son of a slave. What's left of a still in the woods out back next to the original pit grill, abandoned now too. Leafy silence, patches of sunlight, two or three picnic tables crowning the bank of a copper creek.

Then a blur of pines as the land opened up and the sun blistered the pavement, the air streaming through his open window no cooler than the rest of the air, just faster. A tarpaper shack with requisite junk cars littering the front yard and a Rottweiler snapping on its chain as Dieter's pickup flew by. He twisted the dial on the radio, looking for something to settle on: fire and brimstone, honky tonk, pork belly futures, then fire and brimstone again, venomous preachers railing against those malcontents who still railed against the war in southeast Asia four years after the fall. He had watched it unfold on TV at his dad's house, helicopters hovering over the rooftops of downtown Saigon while Kissinger, in his Washington office, denied blame. Dieter's father, close to tears, gaping at the screen, ashamed of the country *his* father, in the wake of the horrors of Verdun, had adopted, cherished, loved.

A shallow ditch parallel to the highway and wider spaces between the trees now, aisles of light. Dips and rises in the pavement, dappled shadows, blade of a road severing a patch of forest that Dieter, with his attention to detail, could readily identify: loblolly pine, southern red oak, persimmon.

As he approached the town, low coast fields of red clay gave way to savannas of sandy loam once submerged under ancient estuaries; in the riverbeds, kids still found sharks' teeth polished to an ebony finish by the sea. And now the names of those languid streams flowed through his mind—*Carrabelle, Blackwater, Santa Fe*—while the road unraveled its long yellow cord. Sparse woods punctuated by splashes of sudden color—flame azalea, St. John's wort—then a scattering of homes. Shotgun shacks but bigger homes too, the men who managed the mill or ran the casino staking their claim in the American dream: three bedrooms with two-and-a-half baths and a pool, with a view.

At dusk he crossed a bridge spanning a horseshoe of gunmetal gray water and discovered the town unchanged since the last time he was there, two decades ago, the year he turned nine. The harbor a tangle of masts and riggings, the town plaza dominated, as it was in Dieter's memory, by a statue of General Lee. When the last of the light flamed against the old brick storefronts, it was not hard to imagine, in fact, what Crooked River must have looked like a hundred and fifty years ago, at the height of the boom. Freight cars topped with Alabama cotton offloaded into the holds of those British schooners that would carry the bales, in the dead of night, across the wine-dark sea.

He parked in front of the Gibson Hotel and stepped into the lobby, struck for the second time since he pulled into town by déjà vu. The same chandelier hanging from the same domed ceiling still in need of a fresh coat of paint. Cracked leather chairs circling a badly stained rug, vaguely Persian. Tiffany lamps. A cuspidor. Behind the front desk, an oak cabinet's two dozen cubbyholes held flat gold keys, room-numbered, and Dieter remembered those too, the stamped keys.

Hearing a customer's footsteps approach the front counter, Mr. Gold, the Gibson's aged, genteel manager, shuffled out of the back room wearing a gabardine jacket and a paisley bow tie, an outfit so old fashioned, a fob watch wouldn't have seemed out of place. He offered Dieter a polite, professional smile.

Good evening, sir. May I help you?

A room, please.

Certainly.

Following a quick, cursory appraisal of the solitary traveler and his apparently much used duffel (a military man? a vagabond?) Mr. Gold opened his ledger, frowning in concentration while he worried a finger down the lined pages, as if the Gibson, which was nearly empty, had few available rooms.

And how long will you be staying with us, Mr. um . . . The manager squinted down at the crabbed signature on the rental agreement, unable to decipher the name.

Dieter. It's Dieter.

Ah yes, Mr. Dieter. Sooo . . . how long?

Observing the traveler's hesitation, Mr. Gold swept a twitchy hand through the few remaining wisps of his white hair, unable to hide his concern. A nice looking young man, but one never knew these days.

Perhaps you'd like me to hold the room then, with a credit card?

Cash. I'll pay cash.

The manager's head bobbed up and down. Currency was good.

Checks could bounce. Credit cards could overwhelm their limits.

Of course.

For a week.

Excuse me?

Cash, Dieter repeated. For a week.

Certainly, sir.

As Mr. Gold watched the Gibson's newest guest ascend the shadowy stairwell, he felt a shiver of apprehension. Because something about young Mr. Dieter bothered him. His indecision? His reticence? The manager couldn't quite put his finger on it, but after forty years in the business a man developed certain instincts, a nose for such things. With a shudder he recalled last month's suicide in room 37. By the time the maid discovered the poor man's body, rigor mortis had set in.

2

If Maggie Paterson thought the world was going to end the night a phone call from Colt's lawyer woke her at 4:00 a.m., she was mistaken. She had been dreaming about the apocalypse again—fire, famine, flood—when the phone woke her, but no, the world didn't end, it just added a few new twists to its dire story. Like the three-inch gash above Jimmy Santiago's right eye, that Howard Simmons, in his lawyerly baritone, now described. Or the broken beer bottle Colt had used as a weapon. Oh, I almost forgot, Simmons added, Santiago's right arm? Well *that's* broken too, nearly wrenched right out of its socket.

Maggie rubbed her eyes. While the lawyer droned on about Jimmy Santiago and the latest hyper drama down at the Black Kat Club, she couldn't quite shake the dream—carrying Hunter through the flames, racing toward the safety of the harbor— even though this new nightmare, unlike the other, was all too real. Colt's usually were. Unscarred, her beloved was sleeping it off down at the drunk tank, Simmons reported. There was still, of course, the question of bail, but that would have to wait until tomorrow. And no one knew at this point whether Santiago was going to press charges. Teddy Mink kept a close rein on those boys of his, Simmons said, but this bit of business was pretty damn extreme, even by Colt's questionable standards.

As he filled her in on the rest of the sordid details, Maggie couldn't help but note how pleased the counselor sounded to be telling her all this. She pictured him out on his screened lanai nursing a vodka tonic, gazing across the moonlit harbor. Assault, he sighed, with a deadly weapon, his voice breezy now, as if he were describing the recent heat wave, or the lack of summer rain.

Maggie had been dreaming about the apocalypse ever since she borrowed that book of paintings from the city library and became fixated on *The Scream*. A tingle of gooseflesh had crawled up her arms as she considered the woman on the bridge, her mouth flung open in a howl of terrible fear. In the background, two other figures were also crossing the bridge but for the life of her Maggie couldn't figure out what they were doing there; they seemed to belong in a different painting. The next morning she had shown *The Scream* to Colt, who feigned enthusiasm though she was fairly certain he couldn't care less. To placate her, he'd lingered over the painting, muttering that's pretty good, Mag. Spooky. But even as he pretended to be immersed in Munch's disturbing vision, his eyes drifted over to the hallway mirror, checking his act out. He liked to sneak these looks at himself almost as much as women did when they saw him on the street strutting his stuff, his Lynyrd Skynyrd T-shirts and skintight blue jeans and Saturday night boots, alligator no less. Faux fucking cowboy, as vain as a Hollywood starlet and just about as bright; why, she wanted to know, am I still with him?

Simmons's laconic voice came back on the line, disrupting her reverie by explaining how Colt, after cutting Santiago, had called for an ambulance, hoping Jimmy wouldn't bleed out before the medics arrived. Arriving at the club at the same time as the medics, two cops listened to Colt's rambling account of the incident, his halfhearted confession, before hauling him down to the clink. Where, cross-eyed with drink, he had used his single phone call to contact Simmons, knowing that the counselor would clean up the mess, because that's what Teddy Mink kept him on retainer for. Barely listening now, Maggie stared out the bedroom door at the dark hallway, wondering if the phone call had woken Hunter.

At any rate, Maggie, I'm sorry I had to wake you with all this.

No problem, Howard, I got the early shift today. And you aren't, she thought sourly, the least bit sorry. You fucking thrive on this.

She hung up the phone and went into the kitchen to brew a pot of coffee. At the window she looked out at the pond, grey in the day's first light. Soon she would have to wake Hunter and bundle him up in a blanket and drop him off at Lureen's. Groaning, she took a sip of the steaming coffee and gazed out at the water, the cattails, the canoe. Beyond tears. Beyond caring. Mostly numb.

Because sometimes it just didn't seem worth it anymore. She hated to give in to despair but maybe it would be better if the dream came true. Famine, flood, pestilence—all those cheery scenarios her sister Lureen, born again, cherished. The sinners vanquished. The slate wiped clean.

3

Like many other small southern towns that had once served as a conduit for King Cotton, and then reaped its share of that shameless industry's outrageous rewards, Crooked River remained, at least on the surface, charmingly antebellum. The original town square was ringed by southern red oaks and weathered wooden benches, where pedestrians, depleted by the summer heat, could rest their weary bones. Two walkways crisscrossed the plaza, and from the four corners of that leafy hub, a wheel of streets branched out, dividing the adjoining neighborhoods into pleasant blocks of antiquated Victorian homes that retained, despite the ravages of time, their aura of former prosperity. To a passerby, their trim green lawns reflected in leaded-glass windows that offered beguiling glimpses of sitting rooms furnished much as they must have been a century ago: floral sofas, walnut sideboards, roll top desks.

From the window of his room at the Gibson, Dieter considered the town. In the glare of a late August sun, General Lee, proud and defiant even in defeat, sat astride Traveler. Uncle Billy, the elderly black man who had toiled as the town's official gardener for as long as anyone could remember, strolled down aisles of flowerbeds spaced evenly across the square, watering his petunias. And in a nearby neighborhood, a middle-aged homeowner trimmed his front lawn with a push mower while a housepainter in whites draped a drop cloth over the hibiscus.

But no matter how many petunias Uncle Billy planted to spruce up the plaza or how many homeowners repainted their lap siding, it didn't take long for a casual observer, much less Dieter, to determine that Crooked River had fallen on hard times. The town had never been much of a tourist destination in the first place, its links to Dixieland's colorful history lost on those northerners whose taste for sugar-sand beaches and tall cool drinks drove them further down the coast. And yet, even a burgh as proud as Crooked River was not above a little civic self-promotion. With his photographic memory, Dieter recalled the town's previous attempts to siphon off a few of the travelers racing down Highway 98 on their way to Clearwater Beach. The miniature golf course. The swampy pond where bare-chested men wrestled drugged alligators into submission. The drive-in theater. Four days ago, as he approached the coast, he had slowed down on that once memorable stretch of road, not particularly surprised to discover the miniature golf course abandoned, the alligator pond strangled by hydrilla, and the drive-in theater—where he and his family once watched Sterling Hayden in *The Asphalt Jungle* perish among his beloved mares—open only on weekends now, for swap meets.

Downtown a number of buildings stood empty, For Sale or Lease signs taped to their dusty windows, though there were a few encouraging glimmers of hope too, stubborn businesses that had found a way, in the face of falling profits, to hang on. Like the Delta Café with its greasy chicken dinners served up by brassy waitresses on the wrong side of fifty. Or the Blue Moon Tavern and its jar of pickled eggs, kegs of Pabst Blue Ribbon, and a refreshing lack of ferns. There was the Gibson, of course, in all its faded glory, along with Paterson's Antiques and Keller's Hardware and the former Opera House, which now showed second-run films. To the utter dismay of much of Crooked River's God-fearing citizenry, there was even a new hippie emporium where those who had strayed off the path of righteousness could purchase a Jimi Hendrix headband, the latest album by Led Zeppelin, or a hookah from Katmandu.

And yet despite these game attempts to maintain Crooked River's commercial viability, only the waterfront seemed as vibrant today as it was in Dieter's recollection. He liked to go down there in the early mornings before the heat set in. After a quick shower, he would toss on a pair of worn khakis and an Indiana University T-shirt and descend the Gibson's aged marble stairs. Invariably, on his way across the lobby, he would stop and chat for a few minutes with Mr. Gold, who hovered over the front counter like a kestrel protecting its nest. The lobby was Mr. Gold's kingdom, and no one passing through it escaped his keen regard. Including Dieter, who, despite the manager's initial reservations, had proven himself an amiable, if somewhat secretive, young man.

And how's Mr. Dieter this morning?

Fine, Mr. Gold, just fine.

Looks like another glorious day out there, though perhaps—the manager leaned over the front counter to peek, with a tremor of disdain, at a nearby sidewalk already flooded with morning light—a bit sticky?

Well, not *too* sticky I hope.

Mr. Gold's placid smile never wavered.

Yes, well, there's always the beach for that eventuality, ay? Christopher Key is it? The one you're so fond of?

I applaud your memory, sir.

With a slight bow, the manager graciously accepted Dieter's compliment. He was dressed today in a seersucker suit and a sky-blue tie. Catching the light, his bifocals glittered.

The fact of the matter, young man, is that it behooves someone in my position to take a certain amount of, um . . . interest in his guests. This is not, as you know, the Holiday Inn.

It certainly isn't!

To anyone overhearing this conversation, the odd, stilted formality of the two participants might have sounded peculiar, but over the last four days, Dieter had come to understand that this was the kind of seemingly innocuous dialogue Mr. Gold preferred, and as one of the few long-term guests currently staying at the Gibson, he was happy to oblige. Even Mr. Gold's gentle but insistent probing—Christopher Key is it?—didn't particularly bother him, though he strongly suspected that his reluctant replies provided fodder for the gossip the manager surely engaged in as soon as his guest was out the door. He imagined Mr. Gold and Consuela the housekeeper trading notes. Consuela in particular would be intrigued by any juicy tidbits Mr. Gold might scatter her way, as she was the one who rummaged, daily, through Dieter's belongings, searching for clues.

After grabbing a coffee to go at the Delta Café, Dieter took up his perch on the seawall that separated the sleepy town from its raucous harbor. Invigorated by the briny air and the Delta's robust coffee, he watched a swarm of deckhands fit out their boats for the day's labor, checking nets for tears, filling coolers with sandwiches and root beer, chopping bait. If they weren't too hungover, the deckhands bantered with their compadres on nearby ships, shouting out increasingly fierce insults or placing friendly wagers on which vessel would catch the most fish that day. Meanwhile the fleet's stern captains moved purposefully about the bridges, their thoughts on the latest weather report—tropical storms could blow up without warning this time of year—or the fluctuating market prices for the bounties of shellfish they would, God willing, haul back to the docks, already on ice, at the end of the day.

All manner of craft crowded the harbor: oyster boats, yawls, dories, shrimp trawlers, that canvas of riggings strung against the morning sky like a classic painting a mariner, in his dotage, might hang on his living room wall. From the bay's clear and unpolluted waters, shrimp and oysters had been harvested for centuries, sponges too, and farther out in the Gulf, grouper, sea bass, reds.

But shellfish remained the mother lode—the oyster boats and shrimp trawlers outnumbering the charters five to one—and most of the fishermen Dieter observed that morning depended for their livelihood on the health of the harbor's beds.

In the muggy afternoons, he drove out to Christopher Key to swim in the warm aqua Gulf. At low tide he could walk out a hundred yards into water no deeper than his ankles, but when the tide finally turned, the shelf gradually deepened, allowing him to dive headfirst into the rollicking waves. Later, lying in the shade of a cabbage palm, he finished the novel he was reading—*Wise Blood*—while munching on the handful of grapes he'd purchased that morning at a fruit stand on his way out of town; Dieter at his leisure until the incessant heat raised beads of sweat on his skin, coaxing him back into the waves. Sometimes he swam to his limit, stroking out past the sandbar, his chest pounding from the exertion and his arms as limp as the sea whips he sometimes stumbled across in the tide's foamy wrack. Back on shore he knelt in the sand, gagging on the saltwater he had inadvertently swallowed paddling back in.

Earlier, on the pay phone outside the lobby of the Gibson, he had called his sister Laurie to let her know where he was, to describe how he had drifted south into the mountains and just kept going, mile after mile, until he ended up here.

Jesus, Dieter, what the hell?

It hasn't changed much, I'll tell you that.

Thanks for letting me know.

Know what?

That you were leaving!

He heard the exasperation in Laurie's voice but how could he have told her when he hadn't known himself? Tell Dad for me, willya? Tell him I'm okay.

The last time he'd seen his little sister she had grilled him good. Was he taking the vitamins she'd sent him? Was he drinking again? Did he ever join the Y? Now, when similar questions elicited the same silent response, Laurie tried another tack. Fine, you don't wanna talk about it, fine. So what are you reading these days?

After a pause he answered O'Connor.

Flannery, right? Not Edwin?

Right, Flannery.

He flopped around in the shallows off Christopher Key, thinking about Hazel Motes in *Wise Blood*. After failing to establish his Church Of Christ Without Christ, Hazel blinded his eyes with lye, tied a strand of barbed wire around his chest, and put broken glass in his shoes. Dieter swallowed another grape. Driven to lesser extremes, Sir Thomas More, he recalled, wore a hair shirt underneath his Renaissance finery.

Well at least that was one thing he didn't have to worry about. Like Hazel Motes and Sir Thomas More, Dieter was a glutton for self-punishment, just not the physical kind. The voice in his head at 2:00 a.m. was torture enough. Besides, he wasn't sure they even *made* hair shirts these days.

4

One evening as he was strolling back to the Gibson after dinner at the Delta Café, Dieter stopped to watch a man on the other side of the street try to wrestle a chifforobe into the darkened interior of Paterson's Antiques. Curious, he crossed the pavement.

'Scuse me. You need some help?

The man bore a striking resemblance to the poet James Dickey, the same wave of white hair, patrician nose, ironic southern mouth. As Dieter approached him, he placed his right foot against the base of the dolly the chifforobe was balanced on and slowly lowered it to the ground.

Matter of fact, son, I believe I do.

With Dieter's assistance the man carefully maneuvered the ungainly wardrobe until it was inches from the entrance of the store. Then, as Dieter held the door open, he coaxed the chifforobe inside and set it down in a slot next to several others.

Frank. The man wiped a large, bony hand on the seat of his pants and offered it to the stranger. Frank Paterson.

Dieter.

Well I surely do appreciate your help, Dieter. Frank stared sideways at the chifforobe with a trace of a frown. Not sure I could have wrangled that in here without you.

Dieter surveyed the room. Cavernous, with a high open ceiling that exposed a puzzle of rafters and beams. Inadequate lighting, all manner of scrappy furniture, and shelf after shelf of odds and ends: decorative tins, musty encyclopedias, glassware.

Encouraged by the stranger's apparent interest, Frank Paterson showed him around the store, pointing out, with an endearing sigh of pride, a fine old secretary desk once owned by a former ambassador to Belgium, a collection of plume hats, a walnut sideboard. On the dusty bookshelves Dieter noted Hemingway, Erskine Caldwell, Ford Madox Ford.

And then, as Frank escorted him past a workroom near the back of the store, Dieter caught a whiff of lacquer and felt the floor sway. The sudden associations triggered by that unmistakable odor were overwhelming, and he had to grab on to the back of a Windsor chair to keep from falling. His father's face, masked by a respirator, as he sprayed the maple cabinets Dieter had stained the night before. Jen wrinkling her nose the first time she stepped foot in the shop: Good God, Dieter, what is that *smell?*

Dieter?

Lost in time, he didn't hear Frank Paterson's voice or notice the look of concern on the older man's face. His hand floated out and nudged open the door to the back room, and at the sight of boxes of rags and cans of stain and reams of sandpaper, the random associations continued; Dieter sanding length after length of mahogany trim while his father shaved, with the blade of a chisel, dovetail joints.

You okay, son?

With a faint smile Dieter nodded at a rocking chair in a shadowy corner of the workroom. The arms of the rocker were stained but the rest of the chair remained unfinished.

You do your own refinishing.

Well, let's just say I used to.

Used to?

The boy that did the work? Took a powder. Just up and left!

A woman, it had to have been a woman, Frank groaned. Or maybe—a long pause, a dark look—it was drugs. He shook his head in dismay. The world was no longer a sensible place. Didn't even pick up his final paycheck! I mean who walks out on a paycheck?

At the front door Frank clamped an affectionate mitt around Dieter's shoulder and gave it a firm squeeze. Thanks again, son. And you all come back some time, hear? We'll set a spell.

Set a spell. In his room at the Gibson, Dieter slumped down in the ratty upholstered chair he'd placed next to the open window, nursing a glass of whiskey. He tried to remember where he had heard that quaint phrase before, and then it came to him: a seedy neighborhood in the village in Quintana Roo where he had lived in his early twenties. Walking back one afternoon to the apartment he rented above the dive shop, he had taken a wrong turn. Late sun scorching the cracked sidewalk blazed in the windows of a row of modest homes. Nearby, a car horn blared, and Dieter hesitated. Was he lost? Earlier, at the Yucatan Café, he'd slammed back several shots of tequila so he was feeling a little queasy now, and the heat didn't help. As he spun around, looking for a recognizable landmark, he noticed a middle-aged man sitting on a front porch stoop, carefully eyeing him. The man was an American, a local gringo who sometimes stopped by the restaurant, where Dieter worked as a prep cook, for a plate of rice and beans. With a nod in the gringo's direction Dieter turned west, toward the falling sun, but after a few tentative steps he suddenly stubbed his toe—he was wearing soft tennis shoes—on a concrete block, that someone, for some reason, had placed in the middle of the sidewalk. He yelped like a small dog and then the man on the stoop was standing next to him, holding his arm. *You better take a load off, son. You better set a spell . . .*

Dieter nursed his whiskey. If he drank the rest of the bottle tonight and took one of the blue pills he might be able to sleep.

At least the day's insistent heat had finally lifted—that would help—and the wind was picking up too, wafting off the harbor into the open window of his room.

Mexico. Nights when the moon rose orange as a rotten melon over the slough. The river was sluggish, the village alongside it little more than a grid of dusty streets, a handful of shabby neighborhoods, and a single hotel catering to the divers who came for the reef. It wasn't much to look at, but in the counterculture enclaves of America, the village had developed a reputation for sexual promiscuity, pristine beaches, and primo weed. Best of all, you could live there on next to nothing, working part time on the dive boats or as a housekeeper at the hotel.

And so expats like Dieter had trickled in, gathering at the Yucatan Café to drink and flirt and swap stories of the road. At dusk, they played guitars and harmonicas and built bonfires on the beach. They smoked a little dope and watched the sun dissolve in the water and talked about whatever popped into their heads, however erratic or profane. What they *didn't* talk about—not much at any rate—was home, as if to seal an unspoken pact to plunge headfirst into the future by denying, as if such a thing were even remotely possible, the past. The Vietnam vets, languishing yet again on the shores of another foreign country, were especially enamored of this attitude. Live for today, they said, or the past will catch up with you. That was their mantra, because in *their* minds the past represented Satan, bloodletting on an unimaginable scale. When the war came up in conversation the vets kept quiet, or silently shuffled away. Only one of them, a kid named Parrish who had spent two years deep in the bush, encouraged by Dieter and his friends, shared what he had seen over there, what he had done, the stuff of his nightmares. Parrish kept a packet of photographs in a black leather satchel and sometimes showed them around when he was drinking. Everyone but the other vets recoiled in horror: dead babies, fire-clouds of napalm, a necklace of human ears. If this was a form of expiation, Dieter thought, Parrish was doomed.

At the Yucatan Café the expatriates bartered trade, a carton of French cigarettes Parrish shipped back from Saigon for a few buttons of peyote, a crate of tomatoes for a stolen macaw. Unless you were out on the water, the days slipped by in a glare of heat but the evenings were long and tribal. Steady drink, a spontaneous rendition of *Norwegian Wood*, tears of joy or sorrow depending on what drug you had just consumed. In the kitchen of the hotel where the divers stayed for a week or two to explore the outer reaches of the reef and sample the local smoke, Dieter slashed open chickens and diced the meat. Rice and beans, the sweet peppers he cored and cut down the middle for *rellenos*. After work he strolled over to the Yucatan Café, hoping Jen would be there. Stoned, he studied the photographs Parrish fanned open on the bar then stumbled out onto the dark sands, terribly lonely. He thought about Indiana, his father, and Laurie. He wondered what he was doing in Quintana Roo, and how long he would stay. And then on yet another otherwise unremarkable Tuesday evening, the purpose was revealed: at the bar, Jen slipped her arm inside his and leaned her head against his shoulder.

In his room at the Gibson, Dieter chased one of the blue pills with the last finger of whiskey and lay down on the bed. A few minutes later he was back in Quintana Roo. From the crest of a hill he gazed down at a moonlit beach where Parrish, kneeling over a small fire, burned the photographs he had taken in Vietnam.

5

As he drove back home from his meeting with Teddy Mink on Christopher Key, Colt brooded. Deep, black, primal brooding; lacerating thoughts. He had been the target of Teddy's wrath a few times before but never like this, and he wasn't sure how he was going to respond. He gunned the engine of his gold Camaro, racing across the causeway, seething. He wanted to break something, to smash something to pieces with his bare hands, to roll open his window and scream. But what good would that do? Reminding himself that it was precisely this—his uncontrollable rage—that had gotten him into trouble in the first place, he eased his foot off the accelerator and slowed down. Taking a deep breath, he glanced out the window at the harbor lights sparkling in the dark, but even that familiar tableau—the ships, in silhouette, rocking on their anchors—failed to calm his rattled nerves.

Turning onto Pheasant Hill Road he pictured, once again, the scene out by Teddy's pool. It had been, in a word, abhorrent. For not only had Teddy given him a major tongue lashing—*that* he had expected—to add insult to injury, he had also done what a man in a position of authority should never, in Colt's opinion, do. He had let one of his bimbos witness the humiliation. To a bouncer like Colt, strippers were a dime a dozen, they came and went, leaving little or no lasting impression, but it would take a long, long time for him to forget the look of amused derision plastered across Nicky Meyers's face when Teddy announced that he was giving Colt one last chance. As if some two-bit hustler who gave dirty old men lap dances had any right to pass judgment on a guy like him. On the other hand, he had to admit that it hadn't been Nicky's fault, exactly; Teddy was the one who had invited her to watch Colt squirm. It was a power play. Occasionally, the boss liked to show one of his minions what it would be like if they ever tried to cross him.

A few miles north of town he turned into a gravel driveway camouflaged by two ragged towers of pampas grass, and wound back to the cabin he and Maggie rented in the woods.

She was waiting at the kitchen table, furiously smoking a cigarette despite having announced, two weeks ago, that she had quit.

Well?

Colt opened the refrigerator and grabbed a can of beer. Well nothin'.

Great. You cut up a friend and spend a night in jail and get bailed out by your boss's sleazy lawyer and that's all you have to say? Nothin'? Maggie took another angry puff of her Marlboro. So you still got a job? You still a bouncer?

Yeah, I'm still a bouncer.

Still a mule?

Colt set his beer down on the kitchen counter, trying to remain calm. Don't say that.

Don't say what?

That word, mule. I don't like it.

Maggie stabbed out her cigarette, beside herself now. And you think what, that I do? Say, what's your boyfriend do for a livin', Maggie? Oh he's a mule, didn't you know? He's one of Teddy

Mink's mules.

Colt took a long swallow of beer as Maggie stormed out of the room. A minute later, hearing the spray of the shower, he walked down to the end of the hallway to finger open Hunter's door. Inside, the kid was already asleep, his face in repose turned toward the glow of a nightlight. Colt padded quietly across the room and leaned over to rub his son's shoulders, careful not to wake him. Then he sat down on the side of the bed. His legs felt like water and he was afraid he might cry, even though the notion of tears was too absurd to dote on. When was the last time he cried?

Later, following a tense, silent supper, he went outside and lifted the battered red canoe from the rack next to the cabin. A harvest moon in a mirror of black water, the stars on their orbits, the idle splash of an oar; on any other evening rowing out across the pond like this would put the world into perspective. For a few minutes, under the starlit sky, his worries would disappear. But tonight, even out here, his mind continued to whirl.

When he arrived at Teddy's palatial estate on Christopher Key, he had been pleasantly surprised by the boss's reception. At the front door, Teddy had shaken his hand. C'mon in, buddy. How you doin'?

I'm all right, Teddy. I'm okay.

How about a drink?

That'd be great.

Scotch, right? Neat?

On the rocks, please.

On the rocks it is. Hey, how 'bout we go sit by the pool. It's a little cooler out there.

Taking a sip of Teddy's excellent triple malt scotch, Colt began to relax. Maybe this wasn't going to be so bad after all. Cutting Jimmy Santiago had been a bonehead move, a terrible mistake, but hey, who didn't make mistakes? He watched Teddy place his own drink, a gin and tonic, on the glass top table that separated their chairs. Dressed for leisure—denim shorts, muscle shirt, flip flops—

Teddy slipped his sunglasses on and stretched out his bare legs. He asked about Maggie and the kid, even remembering that this was the year Hunter was scheduled to start peewee baseball. Then he gave Colt a thumbs up. Chip off the old block, huh Dad?

He's a great kid, Teddy.

'Course he is! Teddy lifted his glass in a toast. Parents like you and Maggie? 'Course he is.

And then as their glasses chimed in midair Teddy presented Colt the full glare of his unreadable smile before inquiring, out of nowhere, without segue, By the way, guy, I was wondering why you cut up Jimmy Santiago like that.

Colt froze, then shuddered. What could he say?

Jesus, Teddy, I'm sorry, man. I'm really fucking sorry.

'Course you are! But that doesn't answer my question, does it. I mean why would you go and do something like that, cut up a friend? Why would anyone in their right mind do that?

In the ensuing silence the only sound was a tinkle of ice in Colt's glass, a hand tremor. Out past the pool, across the flat white sands, silent waves rolled in.

I'm sorry, boss, I don't know what to say.

Then don't say anything!

Teddy, Colt observed, was in fine fettle today; nothing pleased him more than this kind of confrontation. He swooped Colt's glass off the table—Let me top that off for you, buddy—and stood up, his six-foot shadow slicing across the redwood deck. Now that he was a kingpin with nobody in particular to answer to, Teddy had let his blond hair grow out surfer style, a fashion statement which seemed to Colt, no stranger to vanity, faintly ridiculous, considering the man's age.

Was the worst of it over? Teddy Mink was, if anything, unpredictable, but Colt had the feeling that this might be his lucky day. There would be a tongue lashing of course; that was to be expected. He would probably make Colt promise to apologize to Jimmy the next time he saw him, as if they were two kids who'd just gotten into a little scrap in the schoolyard, but that was to be expected too. And then everything, he suspected, would return to normal, as it usually did. He could hear Teddy describing the next run down to the Keys, filling Colt in on the details, where to pick up the rental car and how much weight he was going to carry and who the contact would be. Business as usual. Because when all was said and done, Teddy still needed him, just like he needed Jimmy, to keep the peace at the Black Kat Club and to haul the merchandise down to the Keys. Who else could he count on to move that much product?

He looked out past the pool at the wide sweep of the beach. On the incoming tide a lone surfer rode the crest of a wave while a pelican corkscrewed into the surf, bobbing back to the surface a few seconds later with a small fish in its comical beak. Yeah, Colt was sure of it now, everything was going to be fine. He stretched his arms up over his head and twisted his torso to work the kinks out, back in his comfort zone again.

And then Teddy stepped out the back door with his cat-ate-the-bird grin and there, on his brawny arm, was Nicky Meyers . . .

He dragged his paddle through the water, heading for the far cove. If this were a river he'd just keep going until he was so far away no one, neither Maggie nor Jimmy Santiago nor Teddy Mink, could reel him back in. He'd start a new life somewhere, down in Mexico or Guatemala or old San Juan. Change his identity. Fabricate a fictional past.

You know my man Colt here, don't you Nicky?

Nicky had played it cool, her voice low and throaty. Sure, Teddy, I know Colt. Who doesn't?

Exactly! Teddy cried. Colt Taylor, man about town. Teddy turned to gaze for a few moments out at the distant, scalloped waves, and when he spoke again his voice was so soft Colt could barely hear him. Man about fuckin' town.

Nicky, Colt noted, was dressed in typical bimbo gear, cutoff jeans and a Florida State T-shirt stretched tight across her silicone twins. Designer shades, silver earrings, and plastic, for crying out loud, slippers. With an inauthentic smile she wiggled her cute little peach of an ass into one of the patio chairs.

And from that point on, the rest of the day went to hell, as Colt's mother used to say, in a handbasket. At Teddy's gentle insistence Nicky recounted what had happened that night out at the Black Kat Club. How Colt and Jimmy had been drinking hard all evening. How they'd gotten into an argument over a bet. And finally how Colt, when Jimmy made some kind of disparaging remark about Maggie, had exploded.

As Nicky wrapped up the story, Teddy placed a sympathetic hand on her shoulder and squeezed. Thank you, Nicky. I appreciate your honesty. And I'm really sorry you had to see all that. Then he turned back to Colt and his voice was stone sober now.

I gotta tell you, man, when I went out to the club that night this young lady here—he reached over and patted Nicky's shoulder again—was downright shaken. All the girls were. I mean bloodshed? Paramedics? Cops?

You gotta understand somethin', buddy. What I'm trying to do is run an honest business out there, a clean, safe, honest business. A place where a girl like Nicky can earn enough money she can afford to take those classes down at the community college on her days off.

Teddy removed his sunglasses, as if Nicky's continuing education demanded his, and Colt's, undivided attention.

Did you even know that, Colt? Did you even know that this young lady here is taking classes? Classes! So she can better herself one day.

The boss was on a roll now and Colt knew better than to interrupt him even though he suspected the community college angle was a load of bull. He wished he could lie down on the deck in the sun and go to sleep. Maybe when he woke up this would all be over.

'Course a concept like that, Nicky—trying to better yourself and all—might be a little, well, foreign to a guy like Colt. Teddy leveled his gaze but the mule refused to meet it. He was angry, agitated, on edge. This was an internal affair and should have been handled that way. Bringing the stripper into it was a breach of trust.

Let me ask you something, Nicky. Did you know our boy Colt here was the best damn athlete in his high school class? No? Well he sure the hell was. Star halfback, star pitcher on the baseball team, fucker even knew how to golf! And scouts—I'm talking *major league scouts* now—came knocking on his door one day too, didn't they Colt? Talkin' about his slider.

In utter misery Colt glanced across the table and saw the smirk on Nicky Meyers's face. He visualized how easy it would be to reach over and wipe that grin off for good. One night at the club he had turned Nicky down, and now this, he supposed, was his payback. She had been drinking more than usual that evening and was primed for some action and Colt, it seems, had caught her roving eye. To soften the blow, Colt had assured her that she was the foxiest dancer in the club and that there was nothing more he'd rather do than take her into the back room and bang her silly. But he couldn't do that, he explained, because he had Maggie to think about, and the kid.

Turn 'em down once, just once, and they never forgive you. Ever.

He cradled the paddle in his lap and let the canoe drift aimlessly across the pond. The moon had slipped behind the treetops, darkening the lake, and as he tilted back his head and closed his eyes he saw Teddy take a sip of his gin and tonic.

Yes ma'am, truth is there's a lot more to Colt Taylor here than meets the eye.

Nicky sensed that she had a role to play here, that she was more than just eye candy today, so she spoke up. That right, Teddy?

That's right, Nicky.

Colt waited, in silence, for this to end, hoping that the worst of it was over. Waited until Teddy, without warning, suddenly flipped over his hole card to reveal, to the mule's astonishment, his black ace.

Take his dad, for instance.

Colt's eyes cut across the table and his heart began to pound. Don't do it, he thought. Don't you dare fucking do it.

Colt's dad . . . Well you just aren't gonna believe this, honey, but Colt's dad? Why he was a cop! That's right, a fucking cop! Teddy lifted his hands, palms up, in dismay. And frankly, he continued, I can't help but wonder what poor Mr. Taylor, being such an upstanding citizen and all, would make of this mess his son has gotten himself into, cutting up a friend like that.

I don't expect, Nicky replied on cue, he would be too pleased.

And I don't expect so either! Teddy pondered the distant waves, the night clouds rolling in from the west, the lone surfer. Then he paused for a few more excruciating seconds before launching his next volley, basking in the tension, the anticipation of what he was about to say.

But then again, that's one thing our boy Colt here doesn't have to worry about.

Nicky was confused. She was no longer sure where this was going. A sliver of doubt crept into her voice. Why's that, Teddy?

Because Colt's dad, rest his soul, is no longer with us, honey. And now Teddy took off his sunglasses again and stared at Colt without any expression at all.

How was it the old man died again, boy? I seem to have forgotten.

Colt heard his own voice automatically answer the question but it sounded unfamiliar, like it belonged to someone else.

He ate his gun.

Nicky Meyers blanched, but Teddy sure didn't. Teddy shook his head, mimicking sorrow, and repeated, slowly, Colt's reply.

He . . . ate . . . his . . . gun. Damn.

Colt stared out at the distant water and it all came flooding back, that unimaginable day. Sixteen-year-old star pitcher dancing through the kitchen door after baseball practice suddenly stops in his tracks, his legs quaking, his mouth gone dry . . .

How was it the old man died again, boy? It had been the last straw. Whatever Teddy said after that didn't matter because Colt had already checked out. They were just words. They meant nothing. He steered the canoe back toward the dock, wincing at the memory of Teddy's unforgivable betrayal and his own enormous shame.

At the end of his little performance Teddy had dismissed the stripper, who was more than happy by that time to get away. Why don't you go watch a little tube, sugar, Colt and I have something private to talk about now. And as soon as Nicky wiggled back into the house Teddy had softened his tone, informing Colt that he still wanted him to make the next run down to Islamorada even though, as punishment for cutting Jimmy Santiago, he wasn't going to be paid. And Colt had nodded, accepting this, because at that point he didn't really care.

He dragged the canoe up the dewy lawn and lifted it onto the rack. Then he went into the kitchen for a beer and carried it out to one of the lounge chairs arranged in a semi-circle in the back yard. Sometimes the three of them came out here at the end of the day to watch the sun tumble behind the treetops while the water, in the falling light, changed hue. One evening they heard the cry of some animal deep in a stand of white cedars and Colt had to fight off an urge to reach out and place his hands over Hunter's ears, to protect the boy from the knowledge of what that cry meant. Then he realized just how futile such a gesture would be. The strong killed the weak and then they ate them. It was the way of the world and it always had been, and the kid would discover this soon enough.

He leaned back in the lounge chair, draining the rest of the beer and crumpling the can in his hand. And all of a sudden it occurred to him that there was only one possible response to Teddy's treachery. You paid for your sins—just ask his father—which meant that absolution wasn't possible. But at least he knew, now, what he was going to do.

6

Good day, sir! So how's Mr. Dieter on this lovely morning?

Just dandy, Mr. Gold. Good as, well, gold.

Right as rain, ay? With a jaunty backward wave at the beaming manager, Dieter stepped out into the sunshine, startled by his buoyant mood. Days, weeks, months pass by in a fog of indecision, Dieter the sleepwalker going through the motions of his diminished life. And then one afternoon he climbs into his pickup and heads south over the mountains and winds up here. And now this!

Before leaving his room that morning, he had gathered the flurry of notes he'd penned the night before, stacking the random pages on the desk and weighting down the pile with a conch shell. And now, as he skipped along the sidewalk on his way to breakfast at the Delta Café, he had to chuckle at the mental image of Consuela discovering that trove of yellow papers, page after page filled with Dieter's cramped, untidy handwriting. A poor reader, she would certainly be unable to decipher what all those seemingly aimless, seemingly unconnected words and phrases— with a spontaneous poem or two thrown in for good measure—

meant. Dieter wasn't sure *he* could, and he was the one who had written them!

He considered the poor housekeeper's dilemma. In the two weeks Dieter had been staying at the Gibson, Consuela had uncovered a mere handful of frustratingly meager clues. So far, all she knew was that he read a lot of books and kept his room clean and organized, his socks and underwear arranged in separate drawers, his shirts and pants pressed and folded and hung—shirts on one side, pants on the other—in the closet, his valuables stored downstairs in the safe. Occasionally he drank but never, as far as she could determine, to excess, and not furtively either; unlike many of the Gibson's other guests Dieter left his bottle of whiskey in full view. In a fit of pique, the housekeeper swept the floor and swabbed out the shower stall and replaced the sheets on Dieter's bed. Where, she wanted to know, was the pornographic magazine, the bag of marijuana, the bench warrant for Dieter's arrest? It was driving her crazy. The housekeeper's theory, exacerbated no doubt by her own woeful experiences with men in general, and a trio of less than exemplary husbands in particular, was that every man had something despicable to hide. And then this guy shows up. Mr. Clean. Consuela's beady Latin eyes scanned the room again. Where was the bloodstained handkerchief, the stolen jewelry, the loaded gun? And what about women? Where were the babes?

On top of that, if this distressing lack of physical evidence wasn't irritating enough, there was Dieter's spotless behavior to consider also. He was invariably polite, almost courtly, to Consuela and Mr. Gold. Although he didn't seem to have a job of any sort, he was far from lazy: every morning he went for long walks through the nearby residential neighborhoods and then down to the harbor to watch the boats sail out to sea, and in the afternoons he drove out to Christopher Key for a swim. He usually ate breakfast at the Delta Café and dinner at one of the seafood joints down along the water. According to Consuela's best friend, a waitress at one of those cafes, Dieter always ate alone, displayed, for a relatively slight man, a robust appetite, and enjoyed a glass of red wine with his broiled flounder. He preferred a quiet corner table with a view of the water, was quick to compliment the staff on the quality of the food and service, and tipped well.

And that, in a nutshell, was the problem. For all intents and purposes he was perfect. Good looking (that pageboy haircut and those dreamy blue eyes had already triggered in Consuela's active libido a feverish sex dream or two), well mannered, and self-confident without appearing brash. Groomed, but not fastidious; pleasant, but not flip. Unlike Consuela's three ex-husbands, he didn't seem to think the rest of the world revolved around his ego. In fact he didn't seem to *have* an ego. And that was the second problem: trying to pry information out of the man was like pulling stubborn teeth.

Whenever Mr. Gold pressed the issue, Dieter let drop a few intriguing hints. He hailed from a small town in southern Indiana where his father owned a cabinet shop. He had spent some time in Mexico. He had earned a college degree. A tidbit here, a tidbit there, this paltry trickle of information not nearly enough to satisfy Mr. Gold and Consuela's insatiable appetite for gossip, though at least it was a start. And then one recent morning Dieter had startled the hotel manager out of his usual complacency by abruptly announcing that he had stayed at the Gibson once before . . . in 1959. Twenty years ago on a vacation with his family, he said.

So clearly, Mr. Gold informed Consuela later that day, what we have here is a man attempting to rediscover his past. You must understand, my dear, that each of us, every single last one of us, is on a kind of odyssey, a journey back to our roots. Mr. Dieter, I daresay, remembers a time when the world was less complicated, less fragile, less fraught with modern ills. And that time, it seems, is best represented in his mind by those halcyon days he spent here in our modest little establishment twenty years ago.

To Consuela this all sounded a little highfalutin, but who knew? Mr. Gold was a keen observer of human frailty and his interpretations of the curious behavior of certain quirky guests of the Gibson were often spot on. So, when he proceeded to opine that Mr. Dieter was attempting to recreate a lost period of his youth as an antidote to the distinctive whiff of tragedy behind his gentlemanly airs, Consuela latched on to the idea. Because there *was* something charmingly sad about Dieter, an emotional reserve, an inner distance. Eventually her irritation gave way to pity. What in the world had happened to the poor man?

In the housekeeper's eyes, Dieter remained, in other words, an enigma. And the bizarre pile of paper she discovered on his desk that morning provided additional proof. Careful not to disrupt the sequence of the pages and thus risk exposing herself as a snoop, Conseula scanned Dieter's chicken-scratch handwriting, unable to make out more than a handful of words. Finally, in exasperation, she gave up. It was another dead end. For all the good they did her, the notes may as well have been written in Sanskrit.

After she finished cleaning Dieter's room, she lingered for a few minutes at the second-story window looking down on the town. In the central plaza, Uncle Billy knelt in a bed of lantana, snipping off dead leaves. General Lee glared sternly over the rooftops of Crooked River. And on the sidewalk that looped past the plaza and down to the waterfront, Dieter, with an added bounce in his step today, nodded politely at every man, woman, and child who happened this fine morning to pass his way.

7

After a fearsomely hearty breakfast at the Delta Café (banana pancakes positively drenched in maple syrup) Dieter meandered over to the harbor to watch the shrimp boats chug out to sea. Then he walked, at a southern gentleman's leisurely pace, back to the central square and out through the town's handsome Victorian neighborhoods, occasionally removing from his back pocket the small notebook he now carried with him to record his observations. Like the way water from lawn sprinklers resembled, in the morning light, a spray of silver coins. Or how faces behind windows peeked out from the folds of baroque curtains to track the mysterious stranger tramping through their neighborhood again. Sometimes, spotting one of these peepers, he tipped the brim of an imaginary cap the way famous golfers did when they made a birdie three. *Augusta in the spring,* he scribbled in his notepad. *At the Masters, the dogwoods are in bloom.*

Three days after helping Frank Paterson wrestle the chifforobe through his front doorway, Dieter returned to the store. Frank's smile as he escorted his guest into the showroom was as wide and generous as the mouth of a river, and for a moment Dieter was afraid the older man might wrap him in a bear hug, crushing his fragile bones.

Well c'mon in, boy. I was startin' to think you forgot about me!

As if he had spent the last three days preparing for Dieter's return, Frank promptly closed the front door, put up his *Out to Lunch* sign, and over Mason jars of sweet southern tea commenced to describe, in spurts of homespun eloquence that would have done his twin James Dickey proud, the story of his life. Leaning back in a cozy upholstered loveseat, Dieter grew pleasantly drowsy in the afternoon heat while visualizing, like a dream, every minute of Frank's nostalgic narrative. Frank, the child bobber fishing the Apalachicola River or racing through the piney woods half naked, part animal, part boy. High school football and Frank's first genuine crush, a cheerleader named, appropriately enough, since she had yet to be deflowered, Daisy. Daisy was a true southern belle from a proud and dignified local family who, when Frank sailed off to Europe to fight the Battle of the Bulge, wed, to her parents' consternation, a bookie she had met on a day trip to Pensacola Beach. Unfortunately, on their honeymoon the bookie had escorted his bride out to his favorite racetrack where he squandered her father's considerable dowry by the end of the seventh race. It was an auspicious beginning to a sacred union that would last, Frank reported, all of two months, at the end of which Daisy returned, in tears, to Crooked River, admitting her monstrous mistake.

When Frank came home from the war, the now disgraced former cheerleader was bound and determined to snare him once again, but alas, she was a few weeks too late. For Frank had already promised his hand to Janice Rutledge, a nurse he had met at a military hospital in Louisville while recuperating from a series of shrapnel wounds to his torso and upper thighs. In a modest ceremony at a chapel on the outskirts of town, Frank and Janice were married, and remained so to this day. A fine woman, Frank gushed, my soul mate. But then his voice grew quiet and wistful as he confessed how on certain autumn evenings during football season, despite his abiding love for his wife, he still pined for Daisy, recalling in a glow of ardor the cheerleader's magnificent flips and spontaneous handstands. Because the first cut, he practically sang, is the deepest, even though Dieter already knew that, in spades.

Finally running out of breath, Frank shuffled into the back room for two more jars of tea, and when he returned Dieter stood up and looked him square in the eye.

I'll refinish that rocker for you, sir.

What's that, son?

That rocker, the one in the workroom, I'll refinish it for you.

Frank's expression was indecipherable. Confusion? Doubt? Dismay? He's wondering, Dieter concluded, what my angle is. He's wondering if I'm a thief.

Frank set his jar of tea down and stared into the middle distance, as if considering Dieter's offer. But his shrug was a grimace of pain. Trouble is, well I hate to admit this, son, but the trouble's money. I'm kinda strapped right now.

But that's not a problem, Dieter assured him. 'Cause I don't wanna be paid.

Say what?

Paid. I don't wanna be paid.

Frank guffawed. Clearly the boy was having him on. Now listen, son, don't go talkin' crazy like that, you hear? I don't wanna be paid, he scoffed.

But I don't! Look, I'm gonna be in town for awhile and I need something to keep me occupied. I'll come around now and then and do a little work. Refinish that rocker for you, or this tea cart here. It'll keep me busy. It'll give me something to do. When Frank's dark, skeptical expression didn't change, Dieter barged on. Fine. You can buy my lunch, then. When I'm finished, you can buy my lunch.

Your lunch?

Yeah, my lunch. We can eat here in the store or we can go out. Whatever suits you.

He's ready to cave, Dieter thought. He's ready to give in. One more push and he'll topple. I'm gonna be straight with you, Frank, okay? When I was a kid my dad taught me woodworking. He had this amazing shop, you know? All the tools, even a lathe. And one of the things he taught me was how to refinish antiques. It's something I'm good at, and something I like to do. It relaxes me.

Frank nodded, impressed. The kid didn't say much but when he did, he came right to the point. Frank liked that. He foresaw lazy afternoons in the back room waxing poetic about his wartime experiences in Belgium while Dieter the craftsman sanded away. The boy was a hell of a listener. Frank liked that, too.

And so a bargain was struck, and after a preliminary inspection of the workroom, Dieter presented Frank a list of supplies he would need for the first job: mineral spirits, a box of rags, a gallon of lacquer.

Frank held out a hand. Never look a gift horse, his father used to say, in the mouth.

You got yourself a deal, son.

8

The summer she turned nineteen, Maggie's younger sister Lureen met a private pilot from Wichita Falls whose license had recently been revoked when he blacked out from a near overdose of psylocibin somewhere over the pristine woodlands north of Jasper, B.C. At a raucous party in Panama City, the pilot had coaxed Lureen back to his apartment overlooking an undistinguished stretch of white beach, where, on a moonlit balcony, he offered her a vodka martini before describing, in precise aural detail, the sound a Cessna 150 makes shearing off the crowns of Douglas firs. The plane was toast but somehow the pilot survived, and he had the scars to prove it, he told Lureen, unzipping his pants.

And thus began a torrid affair, afternoon sex followed by exuberant episodes of chemical abuse: mescaline, speed, a handful of peyote buttons, and when things got a little too edgy, various tranquilizers Lureen couldn't remember the names of, washed down with shakers of the pilot's incomparable martinis. The sex was divine, and there were times when Maggie's sister thought this might be love. But she was addled, too, and didn't trust her judgment. Still, it was a strange and exhilarating interlude, right up until the turbulent evening the pilot invited two fellow flyboys from a nearby airbase back to his apartment where something happened that Lureen, to this day, was unwilling to talk about, though she hinted, darkly, the boyfriend's consent. Furious, she drove home to Crooked River in a manic midnight rainstorm and never saw the pilot again.

A few months later, a reformed and no longer disconsolate Lureen swore off booze and drugs altogether, and at the end of one of her weekly AA meetings met the man of her dreams. Hi there, the big man boomed, my name's Charley and I'm an alcoholic and I think you, little lady, are hot!

After an extravagant marital ceremony befitting the son of the local owner and editor of the *Crooked River News*, the young couple proceeded to settle down, buying a house near the center of town and producing a healthy baby boy who would be raised, she assured her sister, in the kind of drug-free, booze-free, God-fearing household she wished she had been raised in also, mindlessly dissing poor Mom and Dad. For not only had Charley and Lureen kicked, in tandem, their terrible habits, they had found Jesus to boot.

You should think about it, she advised Maggie. I mean let's face it, hon, you're not getting any younger.

And you, Maggie thought, are? They were sitting in the Delta Café at the end of Maggie's shift at Winn-Dixie, drinking coffee and sharing, with an eye on their figures, a slice of coconut cream pie.

I *have* thought about it.

Lureen lifted a brow. And?

And I don't know how to swing it, okay? It's a lotta cash.

Her sister shrugged. Ask Dad.

Maggie refused to respond. She stabbed at the pie, piercing the meringue. *Ask Dad* was Lureen's stock answer to everything, as if the parental pipeline was never going to run dry. On the other hand, the idea of taking classes at the local community college held genuine appeal. She could learn a trade, become a nurse, or a CPA. How hard could *that* be, doing other people's taxes? In any event, anything, she figured, was better than what she was doing now. Because Winn Dixie was the pits. The shifts were long and redundant, the pay skimpy, and if that weren't enough, the new manager, Cain the Pain, was getting increasingly frisky. Just that morning, in fact, the Pain had pinched her ass again and Maggie was still steamed.

Listen, hon, there's a corn roast down at the church this Friday. Why don't you stop by?

I gotta go, Lureen.

Seriously, drop by.

I'll think about it, okay?

You do that.

On the way home Maggie picked up a bucket of fried chicken because she was too exhausted to cook. Her shift had been brutal, a steady flow of impatient shoppers stocking up for the annual football game between Florida and Florida State. It was the biggest weekend of the year with tailgate parties launched at the crack of dawn going full bore until kickoff that evening; cases of beer, boxes of brats, industrial-sized jars of pickles. By the end of her shift Maggie's feet ached like the dickens and her concentration was shot. With one eye on the clock above the bakery, she accidentally rang up a zucchini as a cucumber and then somehow kept her cool (on the surface at least; inside, she was boiling) when the hawk-eyed customer—one of those coupon-shopping harridans who never missed a trick—threw a hissy fit about the discrepancy on her bill. Thirty-three cents.

As she pulled into the cabin's gravel drive, she saw Colt and Hunter out at the end of the dock fishing for the perch that sometimes gathered at dusk around the pilings, and her heart sank. There was something timeless, something painterly about the posture of father and son standing side by side like that casting their lines into the pond. Dreading what now seemed inevitable, she saw Hunter's tear-stained face when she told him that Colt would no longer be living there. He would be devastated. For despite Colt's considerable shortcomings, Hunter loved his father even more, Maggie suspected, than he loved her. Because the mother represented discipline—somebody had to— while Colt, with his flashy cars and shiny new golf clubs and cherry-red canoe, represented fun.

She called out the boy's name and lifted up the bucket of chicken and Colt turned too, his lips curling into the lazy smile that used to make Maggie's blood race. Catching sight of Colonel Sander's familiar face, Hunter quickly reeled in his line. At the end of his stringer dangled a single pale perch.

Famished, Colt tore open the bucket and grabbed a still-warm leg while Maggie dished out the coleslaw, mashed potatoes, one golden biscuit each. She asked Hunter about school—he had started kindergarten that year—and then leaned back in her chair, bone weary, to listen to a typically convoluted tale about one Timmy Norton, who refused to take a nap today and kept making funny sounds so the other kids couldn't sleep either.

What kind of sounds?

Moos, like a cow. And beep beeps.

Beep beeps?

The roadrunner!

While Hunter rattled on about Timmy Norton, Maggie looked over at Colt, considering the possibility of a truce. Two nights ago she had reluctantly allowed him back into their bed although she adamantly refused his subsequent advances. He didn't complain but she knew he was frustrated and that sooner or later, if she didn't give in, he would go looking for it elsewhere. And for someone who looked like Colt, *it* wouldn't be hard to find.

After dinner, Colt helped Maggie load the dishwasher and wipe down the counters and stuff the empty containers into the trash. He suggested tea, and put the pot on. And then, as Maggie quietly sipped her mug of chamomile at the kitchen table, he reached out to stroke her arm.

Instinctively she recoiled, yanking the arm away.

Christ, Maggie. He bit his lower lip, stifling an urge to fling his mug of chamomile at the far wall.

I'm not ready yet.

Look, it's not like I killed him you know. Besides, I was just trying to protect your honor.

She couldn't believe her ears. My *honor*?

You shoulda heard what he said about you!

You gotta get away from that place.

We need the money.

You could find something else.

Like what?

Like anything!

He slammed his mug down. It was hopeless. You had to pay for your sins but for how long? Without another word he stomped outside and marched over to the dock and stared, in black anger, out at the water. A blue heron was preening in the shallows and the light was falling fast, turning the pond pewter. Soon the stars would blink on and the moon would lift up over the treetops and the perch would nose the surface again, feeding on gnats. He thought about taking the canoe out but decided he was too riled up.

It just wasn't fair, the way she was treating him. God knows he had screwed up before—what about the night he plowed the Camaro into her new flowerbed?—and yet he couldn't remember Maggie ever being this reluctant to let something go. Shivering at the thought he wondered, not for the first time, if she was considering calling it quits. What if he came home one day and found his belongings in a pile on the back lawn? Where in the world would he go? And how would they explain it to Hunter?

He picked up a small rock and flung it across the pond. Fuck it. If she didn't want to spend time with him tonight he'd find somebody who did, even if it was only Gene, the bartender down at the Blue Moon. They were old pals, drinking buddies, former high school teammates who, over the years, had learned to take solace in each other's considerable lack of achievements.

That was it. He'd go down to the Blue Moon and knock back a few cold ones and bullshit with good old Gene. What was the point, after all, of hanging around here?

9

Gene drew a pint of beer from the tap and placed it in front of Dieter.

So what's the haps, D? Whatcha been up to, man?

Refinishing a rocking chair.

A what?

A rocking chair. For Frank Paterson.

No shit. Over at the antiques store?

That's the one.

Gene wiped the counter with his bar rag, frowning. As a rule, the Blue Moon's customers were easy enough to read because drinkers liked to tell bartenders their life stories, no matter how mundane those stories might be. But Dieter was a different breed, the kind of gambler who plays his cards so close to the vest you never get a peek at them. He was invariably pleasant—a genial drinker—but if you pushed too hard, he clammed up.

Paterson's huh. So you workin' there now or what?

Nah, not really. I just like to refinish antiques. Gives me something to do.

Frowning again—something to do?—Gene grabbed the

remote control and switched on a TV mounted next to a dusty shelf of imported liqueurs no one seemed to order anymore. On the screen, two middle-aged men with perfectly coiffed hair were discussing quarterback options, the wishbone offense, and something called a four-three. Dieter had no idea what the two men were talking about, but he didn't let on.

You like football, D?

'Course I do. Who doesn't?

Atta boy.

So who's playing tonight?

The Eagles. The Eagles and the Broncos. No, wait a minute. Gene looked up at the screen. Not the Broncos, the Rams. The Eagles and the Rams. Dieter smiled at the bizarre nomenclature. Eagles, Broncos, Rams. If Jen were here, she'd gently mock the bartender, careful not to give offense, by asking about the Orangutans, or the Jaguars. She'd say, What about the Jaguars, Gene? Is there a team called the Jaguars?

One afternoon Jen and Dieter were lying in twin hammocks strung between palm trees overlooking the beach in Quintana Roo when it came to him, like a revelation. He sat up grinning, shook Jen's shoulder to rouse her, and said Jaguar Moon.

Jen rubbed her eyes with the heels of her hands. What's that?

Jaguar Moon.

She rolled the words over in her mind, trying them on. Then she sat up too. Well that's it then, isn't it.

Is it?

It's perfect!

Later that night they split a tab of sunshine acid and Jennifer fell apart. Crouched in a corner of his room like a trapped, terrified animal, she reminded Dieter of the madwoman in that play he had seen the year before in Bloomington, the one about Jean Paul Marat and the inmates at the asylum in Charenton. He tried to distract her by reciting some poems by Frost, and when that didn't work, by pouring her a cold *cerveza*, which didn't work either; she took a tiny sip of the beer and winced, her throat still dry. Finally he talked her into a walk on the beach. After supper Jen liked to hike with Dieter down the white sands, listening to the murmur of the surf or pointing out, high above the water, the Southern Cross. But not tonight. Tonight she was terribly frightened, and Dieter was distraught. The acid was too potent, a legendary high that could go haywire at any moment, and apparently had. At the very least the tab should have been quartered, not halved. Why had he split it with her?

Glued to the images on the screen, Gene slapped a hand down on the bar in frustration. Then he addressed the man in the striped shirt, as if talking to someone on TV was perfectly normal. C'mon, ref, throw the fuckin' flag! He was holding him! Didja see that shit, D? Didja?

Thorazine could bring you down from a bad trip but Dieter didn't have any. And to complicate matters, the half tab he had swallowed kicked in too, with a vengeance. He stumbled down the beach shivering from sudden chills though it must have been eighty. A bloated moon hovered over the sea and for some reason Dieter thought it was about to explode. Meanwhile Jen squeezed his hand in trepidation, as if they were crossing a minefield. But it isn't a minefield, he thought randomly, it's a beach. Then again, if the moon explodes, gravity will fail and we'll all go sailing off into the cosmos.

Gene's face was red now and he was shouting at the screen. C'mon, chump, tackle the fuckin' guy! Dieter glanced around the bar at the six or seven other drinkers whose rapt faces, like Gene's, were bathed in the television's blue light. Mimicking the bartender they, too, were talking to the TV.

If you didn't have Thorazine you had to sweat it out. Back in Dieter's room Jen curled into a fetal position, embracing the floor. Dieter wedged a pillow under her head and asked if he could get her anything else but she didn't reply, too high to talk now. So he curled into a fetal position also, on the futon. Outside the wind picked up, rattling the windows, and a few minutes later it began to rain. Dieter shivered again, pinned to the futon by the torque of the drug. Gruesome images raced through his mind, the sacrificial altar at Chichen Itza, a dead dog on the side of a road, his grandfather's tombstone. He felt his body disconnect and float toward the ceiling until there were two of him, the one on the futon apparently asleep and the one in the rafters gazing down at Jen curled on the floor humming a lullaby a mother might sing to a child who had just woken from an ominous dream.

Then a commercial came on; halftime. Gene offered him a wry, weary smile, like a man who had just finished a strenuous workout.

You ready for another one, D?

Right on, Gene.

Old Blue?

You bet.

Old Blue. That's what they called it back home, not Pabst, not Blue Ribbon, but Old Blue. When he was a kid, his dad used to take him to Mallory's Tavern for lunch, and that's what the old-timers would say. Gimme an Old Blue, willya Mac?

Trapped in the acid's steely grip, Dieter was having difficulty breathing and he wondered if his lungs had collapsed. Eventually he lost track of time, but in comparison to not breathing this seemed like a minor development. Was it midnight, 2:00 a.m., a day later? He glanced down at the floor, relieved to discover that Jen was still there and that she had apparently crossed over some kind of psychic divide, her fear coalescing into sorrow. If it was nearly dawn—and the view out the window seemed to confirm this—then they had already peaked and they would begin the slow freefall now. The despair on Jen's face was heartbreaking, but at least she was safe.

He scanned the room. Spotting a stack of albums on the floor next to the turntable, it occurred to him that music might be the best antidote for Jen's emotional distress. So he grabbed hold of the arm of the futon and stood up to cross, on sea legs, the wobbly floor.

So whatdya think, D?

About what, Gene?

The game!

Dieter tried to formulate an appropriate response. He had never been much good at this kind of macho banter but his imagination was creative and rarely let him down.

I'll tell you what I think, Gene. He raised his voice for emphasis. I think those fuckin' refs need an eye exam, that's what I think. Gene slammed his fist down on the bar, maniacally grinning. His deepest desire at that moment was the simple assurance that Dieter was, after all, just one of the boys. Goddamn right they do!

Dieter flipped through the albums until he found the one he was looking for. He slid the record out of its sleeve and placed it on the turntable and carefully set the needle down in the fifth groove. And there, all of a sudden, it was, the piano's first lovely phrases—solemn yet airy, pastoral, light—grounded, moments later, by the bass.

Hearing the music, Jen unfolded her body and sat up. Her face was so puffy and sallow Dieter wanted to flail himself, like Hazel Motes, for feeding her the drug.

What is that, Dieter?

What's what, hon?

That song.

It's called "Jokes Are for Sad People."

In a reverent voice she repeated the title. And then she began to cry.

Dieter held her for a long, long time, rocking away her tears. Then the song ended and the next one came on and in a quiet, muffled voice Jen asked him the name of the band and Dieter answered Fever Tree, they're called Fever Tree.

The band's name seemed to amuse her, which made Dieter's heart leap. It was over. They would crash now, eat a little breakfast, and sleep. Outside, the rain had finally let up, and the moon, paled by dawn, appeared in its quadrant again and Dieter knew that it wasn't going to explode after all, despite his earlier paranoia. It was going to rise and fall, night after night, over the sands of Quintana Roo and the cornfields of Indiana, and eventually over a tavern in Crooked River where men talked to television sets and Dieter sat alone at the end of the bar, mourning Jennifer.

10

The moment he entered the tavern Colt paused, his gaze raking the room for possible enemies. You could never be too cautious, and you could never let down your guard, and yet as far as he could determine the Blue Moon was safe tonight, Gene washing glasses while the usual suspects gaped, like zombies, at a football game on TV. There was a stranger at the end of the bar who appeared harmless, late twenties with a Beatle's pageboy haircut, an Indiana University T-shirt, and a nonchalant expression that might mean anything at all. Good looking, if poorly dressed, but not a threat, Colt concluded, definitely not a threat. He chose a stool two down from the stranger's, greeted Gene with one of those bizarre choreographed handshakes—an elaborate sequence of high fives and fists bumps followed, at last, by a manly thump to the chest—and ordered a draft beer.

Dieter contemplated the new customer, intrigued by his elaborate outfit, the sharply creased jeans and checkered western shirt with pearl buttons no less, and that outlandish white Stetson. Clearly a clothes hound unashamed of his vanity and well aware of the impact he made walking into a room even if there wasn't a single female in the Blue Moon tonight to admire his élan; because men stole glances too, suspecting that this was the kind of guy their wives thought about when they made love. A real peacock with a tense look in his eyes indicating, no doubt, a trigger temper. Dieter took out his notebook and wrote *a peacock with claws*, and when he looked up again Colt was staring at him hard, questioning the notepad.

Then the two Mexicans walked into the tavern and Colt's attention was drawn elsewhere.

One was tall and slender with a drooping Zapata mustache and lank black hair. His companion, short and barrel-chested, wore a Yankees baseball cap and appeared to be the point man, the decision maker. Placing a five-dollar bill on top of the bar he signaled Gene with two upraised fingers before waddling across the room and sliding into a booth directly behind Colt and Dieter, waiting for the tall one to bring the beers.

After placing the bottles on the table, the tall one slipped a quarter into the jukebox and played a song by Bob Seger while his companion tipped his baseball cap back, took a long swallow of beer, and met Colt's gaze in the mirror behind the bar. He opened his mouth to say something to his companion and Colt glimpsed the gleam of the gold tooth and recognized him from the Black Kat Club. His name was Raul and he was Jimmy Santiago's cousin, a notorious badass with a rep for bare-knuckle combat mastered in the back streets of Guadalajara when he was a boy.

Raul took off his baseball cap, scratched his head, and put it back on. His dark eyes remained fixed on Colt's reflection, and when he began to speak he made sure his voice carried across the room.

A broken bottle. What kinda shit is that, *camarada*?

Taking a seat, the tall one remained silent, letting his friend do the work. Macho shit, Raul continued, that's what kind, macho bullshit.

Nodding, the tall one turned around to look into the mirror also and his eyes were just as flat as his friend's, just as unfeeling. Dieter watched the muscles in Colt's face grow stiff and he understood that even though the Mexican was ostensibly addressing his *compañero*, the words were aimed at Colt, and that there was some kind of history here Dieter wasn't privy to.

Fucking Jimmy, man. I hear he had to have one of those what do you call its, they stick the needle in?

The tall one's voice was tight, more confined than his partner's. Transfusion.

That's right, one of those transfusions. It's what you get, when you use a fucking bottle. What you get when you coldcock a guy.

Out of the corner of his eye Dieter saw Gene reach down below the counter to grab something. At the same time Colt stood up and turned toward the two Mexicans but Dieter had already made his move, blocking the mule's path. Adrenaline flooded his body, a strange surge of joy.

The tavern fell silent. In the old days Dieter would have frozen at that moment but fear died one night on a rainy highway outside Bloomington. Now, in the face of physical danger, he just didn't care. He lifted his hands to show the two Mexicans his lack of weapons. *Buenas noches, amigos. ¿Como estan?*

The tall one seemed reluctant to answer but Raul was not so bashful. *Buenas noches, señor.* Emboldened, Dieter started across the room, mouthing an apology. *Disculpe, no quiero molestarle.*

Raul shrugged—*No es ninguna molestia*—it was no bother at all. His gold tooth gleamed again, reminding Dieter of one of those Mexican bandits in American westerns who smiled like that right before he unsheathed his machete and cut off the gringo's hands. *Gracias, amigo.* Dieter pointed at the Mexicans' beer bottles, which were almost empty. *¿Dos cervezas mas?*

Raul lifted his palms in surrender; if the gringo wanted to buy the next round, who was he to disagree? So Dieter turned back to the bar and said three beers, Gene, and three shots of tequila, and the bartender gladly let go of the billy club he had been holding on to for dear life. In the two years he had worked at the Blue Moon he had been forced to brandish the club three times but never, thank God, to swing it.

Cuervo?

Let's make it the good stuff. Dieter pointed at the top shelf. Give me the clear. And three Buds, please.

Later, when Gene reconstructed the evening, he would swear Dieter winked at him at that moment, as if sharing some kind of private joke, before focusing on Colt, who was still standing next to the bar watching the two Mexicans.

How about you, friend? Ready for another beer?

Keeping Raul in his peripheral vision, Colt considered the offer, but not for long. I don't think so, pal. Reckon I'll buy my own. Picking up his glass, Colt sauntered over to the end of the counter and sat down on a stool with a clear view of the Mexicans' booth. He wasn't about to turn his back on Jimmy Santiago's cousin but he wasn't leaving the tavern either. This was his local watering hole, and no one was going to scare him away.

Dieter set the bottles of beer on the Mexicans' table and returned a minute later with the tequila. Still smiling, Raul patted the seat cushion.

Por favor, señor, como en su casa.

Raul raised his shot glass—*a su salúd*—and Dieter and the tall one repeated the toast, to your health, clicking their glasses in midair. Then Dieter slammed the shot back and chased it with a swig of beer, his hand steady, his nerves calm. He let the silence build for a few minutes to show them he wasn't afraid, a trick he had learned in Mexico. Like boxers, you met in the center of the ring and you didn't blink, you never blinked.

De donde es usted?

Raul waited a beat before replying, as if considering whether he should.

Guadalajara.

Ah *sí*, Guadalajara. *Lo conozco bien!*

Dieter recalled, with an ache, the old town. Dusk. In the zocalo, a shoeshine boy polished a tourist's jet-black shoes while a group of musicians gathered in the shade of a fig tree to tune their instruments. The sun plunged over the steeple of the grand old cathedral and then the shadow of the steeple inched across the square, spearing the walkways, as Jen took Dieter's arm. They stepped into an elegant café just off the plaza, where the proprietor, an old man with a cloud of white hair who remembered Jen from the old days before Quintana Roo, pecked her on the cheek and clasped Dieter's right hand in both of his. Calling out to one of his waiters, he escorted them to a corner table, Jen's favorite, with a view of the courtyard's gurgling fountain and caged macaw.

Dieter named the restaurant and Raul's expression softened, for he remembered it too. And when Dieter began to describe, in great detail, the extravagant feast the old proprietor had prepared for them, Raul and his *compañero* leaned over the table, impressed by the respect the gringo, in excellent Spanish, paid to their native cuisine. Dieter's narrative had brought their hometown back to them, and in gratitude Raul refused to let him pay for the next round, placing a twenty on the table and making sure that Gene picked it up when he came over with their next tray of drinks.

Now that he had the Mexicans' attention, Dieter made his pitch, lowering his voice and speaking this time in English. I do not know, my friend, what the trouble is between you and the man at the bar, but I know it is none of my business. He let that sink in for a few moments. Unless, that is . . .

Unless? The word seemed to pique Raul's interest.

Unless you choose to tell me.

Taking his time, Raul lit a thin, slender cigar, watching the smoke curl like a question mark into the stale air. I see.

Jimmy, for instance. Would Raul be willing to tell him who Jimmy is?

The two Mexicans exchanged a look and then the tall one replied, in his rasp of a voice, he is Raul's cousin.

On his father's side? Dieter asked.

Sí, señor, pon parte de su padre.

Dieter sipped his tequila, introspective now, weighing the

odds. One false move and it could all unravel at once. And now he is injured, no?

Sí, señor.

And the man at the bar, he is the one who cut the cousin?

Behind a veil of smoke, Raul nodded.

Then I understand, Dieter stated, your anger.

Raul contemplated the ash at the end of his cigar. Cutting a man with a bottle, he hissed, is the act of a coward.

Yes, I understand. Dieter chugged the rest of his tequila, throwing caution to the wind.

And yet still I must ask you, with all due respect, for a favor.

Raul lifted his brows, intrigued. What, he wanted to know, would that favor be?

That you take your fight elsewhere. Dieter waved his right hand, indicating the room. This is my neighborhood tavern. This is where I drink. And I like to drink, as I'm sure you do, in peace.

After a long pause Raul took off his Yankees hat and scratched his head. But you misunderstand us, *señor*. We did not come here to fight. He pointed at the TV. We came here to watch the ballgame.

Which might, Dieter thought, be true. Then I am pleased, he said, that you did. In fact, I am honored. I am very fond of your country. I miss it a great deal.

As do we, *señor*. As do we.

Eventually, three more rounds were consumed before Raul and his companion rose, a little unsteadily, to their feet. They shook Dieter's hand and said *sí*, they would be pleased to have dinner with him down on the docks one night. And then halfway to the door, as if it were an afterthought, Raul wheeled around and raised a thumb in the air and pointed his index finger at Colt, pretending his hand was a pistol. Taking aim, he squeezed off a round, a gesture Colt, in disdain, refused to acknowledge. The blood feud was far from over but it wasn't going to end tonight.

At the bar, Dieter twirled his empty shot glass, his eyes a little unfocused now. You know I used to drink this cactus juice like it was water.

Shit'll kill you, man. Shaking his head, Gene grabbed the shot glass and set it in the sink. Now more than ever Gene was determined, like Consuela, to crack the Dieter code.

That was some kinda chatter, D. Where'd you learn to talk Mex like that?

Dieter let the question hang for a minute before answering, in a quiet voice, Mexico.

That right? Spend some time down there did you?

Some.

Yeah? Like where? Cabo? Cozumel?

Ah, you know—Dieter shrugged, giving nothing away—here and there. He rapped his knuckles on the bar. Look, I gotta go. While I still can. I'll catch you later, okay?

Colt waited for Dieter to disappear out the door before turning back to the bartender, baffled. What the fuck was all *that*, Geno?

Damned if I know.

Strange cat.

Dude's a paradox, man. An enigma.

A paradox? An enigma? Colt frowned at his old friend. What the fuck, bro, you been readin' books again or what?

11

The days drifted by in a glaze of heat, though the mornings were incrementally cooler now, particularly down along the harbor where gusts of wind rippled the sails of the pleasure boats anchored in the marina, their hulls at sunrise coated with a thin sheen of dew. Sailboats lying at peaceful anchor, even as those sheltered waters were transformed at first light into a hive of activity, stern captains manning the bridges of their vessels, while the worker bees below them scurried to and fro.

Perched on the seawall that separated the harbor from the town, Dieter flipped open his notebook and wrote, *coated with dew*? He'd have to think about that for awhile, when he returned to his room. Skim a finger down the busy margins of a Thesaurus until he latched on to something better—sheathed?—or decided that *coated* would do. For a rough draft, that is, of a note.

To the deckhands fitting out their trawlers, he had become a familiar figure, the stranger who was staying at the Gibson, strolling past their slips, as he did most mornings, jotting down notes in his pad. Some claimed he was a writer doing research for a book about the fishing industry. Others concluded he was crazy, scribbling gibberish. While still others speculated that the notebook was therapeutic, a daily journal recording the thoughts of a man recovering from some kind of personal tragedy up north, the loss of a fortune or the death of a loved one or trouble with the law. They often spoke to him as they humped supplies from the docks to their boats and he was invariably cordial, inquiring about yesterday's catch or the rumors of a hurricane gaining strength in the lower Gulf. Nights, he favored The Tides, a tavern with an excellent menu down on the marina where many of the deckhands liked to drink.

If Dieter spotted a group in the bar, he would buy a round of beers and encourage them to talk about their work. He was a polite, careful listener, and as the deckhands described their days out at sea, a faint smile crossed his lips, as if he, too, could smell the brine in the air and see the black thunderheads of September blossom on the horizon. And yet, when the deckhands parried Dieter's questions with a few of their own, he steered the conversation in a different direction. He mentioned a town in Indiana called Bloomington and a cabinet shop owned by his dad, but when they pressed him for further details he quietly replied that no, he wasn't married, and he didn't have children either, though he certainly hoped to some day. What about them? Did they have any kids?

Two or three days a week he worked in the back room of Frank Paterson's antique store sanding the doors of an armoire or reattaching a loose veneer. At noon, Frank went over to the Delta Café and came back with paper bags filled with cheeseburgers and coleslaw, onion rings and French fries, slices of apple pie. In between bites he talked about his daughter Lureen and her husband Charley, who one day would inherit his father's newspaper. Then he reached into his wallet to show him a photograph of his other daughter, Maggie, and Dieter heard the adoration in Frank's voice but the pain, too, the disappointment. Frank made it clear that Maggie's live-in boyfriend was not much of a catch, and that even though his oldest daughter could take care of herself—because Maggie, Frank assured him, was what used to be called sassy—he and Janice were worried about the boy. What kind of role model was a bouncer at a strip club for a six-year-old boy?

In the afternoons, Dieter drove out to Christopher Key to swim, cruising past the old abandoned saltworks at the edge of the estuary then turning right onto the key. He favored solitude, avoiding the developed southern end of the island for the unspoiled beaches of the north. From the little-used parking lot, a sandy path strung with chains of morning glory meandered through a grove of sea pines and up over hillocks of dune. Then a hiss of waves and the first sight of the glowing water, a blue carpet woven, here and there, with white threads. In the shade of a cabbage palm he set up a folding chair and unpacked his gear: beach towel, fruit and water, paperback book.

One day on the beachside trail, he encountered a black snake as long as his leg and pulled up short, awed by the size of this serpent. He recalled a water moccasin sliding past his shoulder one day as he swam across a limestone quarry outside Bloomington with Jen. College students came to the quarry to dive off the cliffs or to lie naked in the sun, tanning their backsides, and at first Jen had been too shy to skinny-dip alongside the others. But by the third or fourth visit, she began to worry that her refusal to disrobe like everyone else might be viewed as arrogance, so she finally relented, quickly flinging off her swimsuit before diving off a shelf of rock.

The languid waters of the Gulf were still tepid from the heat of summer unless you ventured out past the sandbar and the safety of the shelf. There, in the deeper water, the temperature abruptly plummeted as Dieter dove toward the sandy floor, kicking his legs against the current until his muscles began to cramp. Back on the surface he swam in long lazy strokes, striking a line parallel to the beach in the draft of an incoming tide that further impelled his momentum. He swam until his arms grew weak and his lungs burned from the flame of exertion. Then he flipped over on his back and floated, allowing the waves to carry him into the shallows and eventually onto the shore, where he dried the saltwater off his skin, peeled one of the oranges he had purchased at the roadside stand that morning, and cracked open the book he was reading now, a novel by Thomas McGuane.

In the late afternoon, thunderheads as thick and dark as beef broth roiled in from the west and the wind quickened in the cabbage palms, rattling the fronds. Dieter had become adept at anticipating the speed of these storms, and he liked to wait until the last minute to gather his gear and jog back to the parking lot moments before the first drops spattered the ground. Driving back into town, he thought about the deckhands out on the water monitoring the approaching clouds even as they winched in yet another fishnet bulging with oysters or shrimp. If the rains came early, the deckhands would gather at The Tides to hoist pints of lager to the vagaries of the sea, refusing to acknowledge how worried they were about reduced paychecks in this season of storms. Sometimes when Dieter strolled into the bar the deckhands called out his name, knowing he would buy the next round even if they insisted he shouldn't.

Once a week, on the pay phone in front of the Gibson, he called Laurie.

What the hell, Dieter. When are you coming home? When he failed to respond, she raised her voice. I want you to listen to me now. Come home.

It's not that easy.

Sure it is. Hop in your truck. Point it north. There's nothing for you down there.

You don't know that.

You may as well be in Singapore. In Spain.

Yeah well, I reckon those are some good places too.

I'm not talking about *places*, Dieter.

Barcelona. Seville.

And neither are you.

He pictured Laurie at her kitchen table with the phone in one hand and a pencil in the other, grading exams.

I've been doing some writing, Laur.

A long silence then Laurie's voice again, subdued now. Yeah?

Yeah.

What kind of writing?

Notes.

Notes?

About the town.

Another long pause. He could hear her fingertips, or perhaps the eraser-end of her pencil, tapping the table. Talk to me, Dieter. Tell me what I need to know.

With an ease that surprised him he described the harbor at sunrise, the abandoned saltworks, the beach at Christopher Key. He told her about Frank Paterson and Consuela the housekeeper and good old Mr. Gold; about the deckhands on the trawlers, Uncle Billy in his flowerbeds, the statue of General Lee. He even related the incident between the two Mexicans and Colt Taylor at the Blue Moon the other evening, deprecating his own integral role in that affair. And when he ran out of breath Laurie gave him a minute to recover before saying, More, Dieter, give me more. So he took out his notebook to read to her what he had written today on the beach at Christopher Key, the way he used to read to her when he was a teenager, tasting the words on his tongue and wondering if some day when he released them into the blind air they might assume a kind of resonance, like birdsong, or wind.

He flipped open the notepad. *That afternoon he crossed over the last mountain pass and dropped down into the valley, into hardwood forest, hardwood swamp. Hill country for the next twenty miles but bottomland too, brackish water the color of iced tea swirling around trunks of cypress, the swamp's oldest trees.*

On cue, Laurie chimed in, co-authoring it the way she had when they were children sharing this, their first great secret.

Slowing down.

Yes.

Taking his time.

That's right.

Avoiding the less traveled roads to satisfy . . . to satisfy what, Dieter?

An urge. An ache.

For real country. In her muted voice, this sounded like a prayer.

Exactly, Dieter said. For real country. For red clay.

12

In response to one of Mr. Gold's gentle, if insistent, queries, Dieter sheepishly admitted that he had indeed polished off his entire order of banana pancakes down at the Delta Café that morning, with a side of fried eggs. Which was why, he declared, it was time for some serious exercise. He patted a belly that remained, despite his robust appetite, washboard flat.

Gotta hike off some of that maple syrup, Mr. Gold.

With a wisp of a smile the hotel manager adjusted his ascot. The subject of food was dear to the man's heart, a portal into the past. Tried the pecan pie yet?

Oh yes.

And the butter, Mr. Dieter, did they remember to put that little pad of butter on top?

They certainly did.

The smile widened, the bifocals glittered, the ascot flamed red against the starched white collar of his shirt. And you let it melt first, right, before the first bite?

I assure you, sir, that I let it melt.

Mr. Gold flushed, as pleased as a proud father beaming down

on his dutiful son. Well that's fine, young man, just fine. You know my mother was the one who taught them that little trick. Did I ever tell you the story?

No sir, I don't believe you did.

Five minutes later, after hearing how Mr. Gold's mother burst into the Delta Café one evening to inform the bewildered owner that he was not serving his pecan pie in the traditional southern manner, with a little pad of butter on top, Dieter patted his belly again, steering the manager back to the present day.

Exercise, you say?

Removing a trail guide from his back pocket, Dieter pointed out the stretch of the Wakulla River he planned to hike that morning, a streamside footpath weaving through a tract of deep, piney woods. He had recently purchased a new camera, he said, and he wanted to snap some photos.

Well now you be careful out there, young man. You carry, I take it, a first-aid kit?

Dieter assured Mr. Gold that indeed he did, concluding that a little white lie was preferable to the truth as long as it tempered the hotel manager's absurd but touching concern.

And a snakebite kit?

Oh yes.

Aloe vera?

You bet.

At the trailhead he parked his truck along a gravel pullout, conducted a quick inventory of his backpack—canteen, camera, binoculars—compared the map in the book to the one on the trailhead sign, and set off.

The air was muggy, the ground still damp from yesterday's rain, but as soon as Dieter marched back into the shadows of the loblolly pines, he forgot, for the time being, about the heat. Strolling along the harbor in Crooked River or the beach on Christopher Key were pleasant enough diversions, but a wood like this was where Dieter felt most at home. When he was a boy, his father had taught him the pleasures of hiking, clearing an old

deer trail that curled back through a tangle of trees behind their
property to a hidden pond where catfish as long as Dieter's arm
swirled the muddy depths.

Half a mile past the trailhead, the path crossed a rickety
wooden bridge and from that point on more or less skirted the
Wakulla River, twisting past quarter-moons of sugary sand
exposed by the sluggish current or occasional cut banks where
the channel ran clear. There were small hills heavily shaded by
live oaks and the air was dense in there, breathless, close. Dozens
of birds flitted in and out of the shadows mostly unseen, though
Dieter could still identify, by their songs, red-winged blackbirds,
some kind of warbler, and a scrub jay. Jen was the one who got
him started, referring to the panels in Petersen's Field Guide as
they hiked a trail behind the house Dieter built for them a few
miles south of Bloomington, not far from his dad's, a leafy path
skirting a narrow stream for two or three miles before the water
plunged into the mouth of a cave so dark and labyrinthine the fish
inside the cave remained albinos, schools of minnows as pale as
summer clouds.

It all came back to him now, the stream spilling over a cairn
of boulders, the cattails nodding in the shallows, the wrens and
sparrows that nested in the dark towers of beech that crowned the
canopy, erasing the sky. And Jennifer, Jen . . . If he closed his eyes
he could see her skipping down the trail into the next clearing,
twirling around like a ballerina as she must have done when she
was a little girl in New Hampshire growing up in the shadow of
the White Mountains, hunting mushrooms, fishing, like Dieter,
with her father, and hiking through woods like these.

Think about it. How lucky we are. You and me, Dieter! She
had flung up her arms, spinning. All this!

Dieter knelt on the lip of a cut bank to photograph the
serrated blades of a saw palmetto but he had lost his focus.
Crushed, he capped the camera lens and slumped down with his
back against the trunk of a tree. *You and me, Dieter! All this!*

After awhile he wiped his eyes with the heels of his hands

and stood up. It was no good now but you had to go on. The days would unwind like clockwork, without meaning, but you had to go on. He cinched the backpack, scraped the mud from his boots on a spear of rock, and set off again. The trick was to think, if possible, about nothing.

A mile later he stopped to consult the map, to confirm that this was the far end of the loop, the juncture where a fork of the river swerved off to the left before draining into a small pond on the edge of the forest, while another tributary circled back to the road.

The heat was oppressive, a blanket of steam. Dieter studied the miniature blue bowl on the map, the unnamed pond, and wondered if it was deep enough to swim in. The weight of the past had induced a kind of lassitude that made him yearn to lie down in the leaves and fall asleep, but that wouldn't do. You had to go on. One way or another you had to go on. Pocketing the trail guide, he opted for the left fork, hoping that a vigorous swim might revive his energy, perhaps even salve, for a time, his broken spirit.

The trees opened up, revealing the boomerang-shaped pond. On the far bank there was a sturdy dock, a trim lawn with a canoe rack, and farther back, a cabin in the woods. Dieter swept his binoculars across the property. When he didn't spot a vehicle in the drive or anyone moving around the cabin he loosened the backpack, unlaced his hiking boots, and stripped off his clothes.

Having finished her morning chores, Maggie shuffled into the kitchen and peeked out the window at the sky, the trees, the reeds in the shallows and the slender bars of shadow they cast. Then a swift cloud passed in front of the sun and in the sudden gloom of that moment she saw, to her astonishment, a naked man on the far bank glance up at the same passing cloud before wading, step by cautious step, into the water. The chiseled body, pageboy haircut, genital thatch: in an instant Maggie took it all in. Transfixed, she watched the man lift his arms, knife the surface, and emerge moments later to swim—gracefully, effortlessly—the length of her pond.

13

One night Colt agreed, or more accurately allowed himself to be coerced, into watching a foreign movie on TV. No fan of subtitles, at first he had balked at the idea of wasting a perfectly fine evening on some dark and depressing foreign film. But when Maggie, who had finally allowed Colt back into her bed, strongly hinted that if he made it through the entire movie she would consider performing that little erotic trick he had recently become so obsessed with, he had finally relented, settling into his recliner with a bowl of popcorn and a cold can of beer just as a soaring helicopter, in the very first scene no less, lofted a statue of Jesus over downtown Rome.

A few weeks before, when her sister Lureen returned from a road trip to Tampa raving about the new art museum she and Charley had visited while they were there, Maggie had decided that her life lacked Culture with a capital C, and so had begun a campaign to correct this oversight by dragging home from the local library coffee-table art books, postmodern novels, and collections of poems. With the passion of a true convert she also scoured the single shelf of the Crooked River video store devoted to foreign titles, determined to watch every last one of them. Thus dreary old Bergman for a solid week followed, tonight, by her first Fellini. Colt hoped it was all a passing fancy, but with Maggie you never knew.

The next evening Colt recalled how strange and confusing the movie had been, what with that flurry of dialogue racing across the bottom of the screen. The only scenes that had held his interest were the ones that took place in the string of nightclubs along the Via Veneto. The grotesque close-ups of the denizens of those swanky joints had reminded him of the sorry patrons of the Black Kat Club, because the air of malaise that hung like smoke over those chic Italian trattorias wafted across the Kat, too, particularly on a humdrum Tuesday evening like this one. Bored strippers going through the motions while the usual crowd tried to rise to the occasion, no pun intended, when the deejay in his glass booth entreated them to put their hands together and extend a warm Crooked River welcome to Bambi, the newest addition to Teddy Mink's ever-growing stable of top-heavy babes. Bambi? Colt shook his head in dismay. What kind of fucking name was Bambi?

Standing at his outpost at the end of the bar where he could monitor both the patrons and the front entrance, Colt allowed himself a brief fantasy. As Bambi coiled her naked limbs around the stripper's pole the front door banged open and there was the great Fellini himself sweeping into the Kat, trailing in his wake an entourage of fans, to film a scene for his next movie. With theatrical flourish the famous director air kissed Colt on both cheeks before inquiring, in broken English, whether the bouncer would be interested in playing a small but key role in the sequence he was getting ready to shoot.

Colt? Outside, the paparazzi whizzed by on their little Italian scooters while Anita Ekberg sashayed past the Kat in a dress that left nothing to the imagination . . .

Colt!

Snapping out of it, Colt glared across the smoky room at Jeb, the night bartender, who was wiping down the counter with a greasy rag.

What?

Closin' time, man, last call.

While Jeb dimmed the lights and counted the cash in his register, Colt collected the last of the empty bottles from the horseshoe counter that surrounded the stage. He thought about *La Dolce Vita*, his first foreign film. Anita fucking Ekberg, man; now there was a real woman. You'd never see *her* humping a pole. He placed the empties in their cardboard cases, conducted a quick tour of the dressing room to make sure none of the strippers had passed out back there, and told Jeb that he would lock up.

At the back door he secured the double lock and flipped on the security switch. He was looking forward to going home and heating up some dinner and watching a late movie, an American movie, on TV. Since he and Maggie had reached a sort of truce—since they had decided, that is, to be civil around each other—he had begun once again to enjoy his time at home.

'Scuse me.

Startled by a woman's sudden voice he spun around, surprised to discover Nicky Meyers, pale as a wraith, standing next to the stage.

'Scuse me, Colt. Can I talk to you a sec?

The bouncer hesitated, unsure what to do. He hadn't spoken to the stripper since that awful day out at Teddy's, and he didn't particularly want to now.

About what?

Please. It'll only take a second.

With a curt, unfriendly nod he slipped behind the bar and grabbed a bottle of Heineken and brought it over to the table where Nicky had already taken a seat.

So what's on your mind, Nicky?

The stripper lowered her eyes, unable to meet his flat gaze. I wanna apologize.

Oh yeah? For what?

For my behavior the other day. Over at Teddy's.

Even when she was offstage, Nicky Meyers tended to project a sense of self-confidence bordering on cocky. But not tonight. Tonight she appeared shy and uneasy and her clothing reflected this change in attitude too, a conservative skirt and blouse replacing the trashy outfits she usually favored.

I didn't know Teddy was gonna pull something like that. It was rotten. I should have said something.

Colt didn't know if Nicky was sincere but she sure *seemed* repentant. He took a sip of his beer, waiting for her to continue.

The way he brought up your father. That was totally uncalled for.

When Colt didn't respond, Nicky forced herself to look at him. Listen, what I wanna say . . . well what I really wanna say is if you ever need someone to talk to, about your dad I mean, or anything else, she quickly added, I'd be glad to listen.

Once again flustered by Colt's refusal to reply, she reached into her purse and handed him a scrap of paper.

That's my number, okay? Just in case, you know, you change your mind. She rose to leave, smoothing her skirt with the palms of her hands. And I hope you'll find a way to forgive me, Colt, I really do.

Colt stared at the phone number, recalling the smirk on the stripper's face the day she witnessed his humiliation. He'd vowed, then, to never speak to her again. And yet now that she had formally apologized he could afford, he supposed, to be generous.

Hold on there, girl.

Halfway to the door Nicky paused, slowly wheeling around. Colt made her wait for a minute, holding her gaze until she lowered her eyes in embarrassment.

Fine, he finally said with a shrug.

Fine?

Fine. I forgive you.

You do?

The relief on the Nicky's face was palpable. Okay then! With a yelp of joy she skipped back across the room, bent over the table, and planted a kiss on his lips, briefly sliding her tongue in. Then she breathed into his ear, *Call me*, and Colt couldn't help himself, he wanted more, he wanted all of it, every damn inch. He contemplated Nicky's exquisite hips as she wiggled toward the door and twirled around at the last moment to blow him a playful kiss. There was no doubt about it, Nicky might be the most histrionic stripper in the club, but this was a side of her he had never seen, a glimpse of vulnerability that gave lie to the brassy persona she projected onstage. She was just as lost, he thought, as everyone else.

On the drive home that night he replayed the scene over and over in his mind. How Nicky had been unable, at first, to meet his eyes; her quiet, respectful voice when she mentioned his father; her prim and proper clothing. By revealing humility and admitting regret she had sunk a hook into his heart and he didn't want to dislodge it just yet. He fingered open his shirt pocket to make sure the scrap of paper with her phone number on it was still there.

As he turned off the highway onto Pheasant Hill Road he saw the flashing emergency lights of a stranded vehicle. A late model Ford Escort was pulled off onto the shoulder of the road and a young woman with a stricken look on her face was standing beside it. As his headlights caught her in their glare, the woman lifted a tentative hand.

Colt parked his Camaro and slid out. He nodded at the Escort.

Car problems?

The stranded driver was a pretty, petite Hispanic with a plume of jet-black hair tied in a long single braid down the middle of her back. *Sí senor.* The engine . . . how you say? Overheated?

With a bit of a swagger—the handsome gringo coming to the rescue of a damsel in distress—Colt took control, grabbing a flashlight from his glove compartment and stepping around to the front of the woman's car.

But as he reached under the hood to lift the latch, something moved in the trees to his left, rattling the dry brush. A possum, he thought idly, or maybe a raccoon. Then whatever it was moved again, and when Colt swung the hood open he realized that the shadow emerging from the woods wasn't an animal but a man.

The gold tooth gleamed in the dark as Colt tried to shield his face with his hands, an instant too late. Before he had time to react, the jagged end of a broken bottle knifed through the air and slashed open his left cheek, down to the bone. His legs collapsed and he fell to the ground and for a few moments the only sound came from the cicadas in the trees. Then the bottle shattered on the pavement and Colt curled into a fetal position even though he knew that this was fruitless. His attacker's fists, and boots, were like pistons. Before he blacked out he heard the woman cry out for the man to stop, but that was fruitless too.

14

After toiling late at the office on a tax-evasion case due to go to court in less than a week, Howard Simmons was at home on his patio mixing the single nightcap he allowed himself on a workday evening—two fingers of Absolut vodka with a splash of Perrier and a slice of fresh lime—when the phone rang.

They found what?

The voice on the other end of the line belonged to Pursley, a precinct captain not opposed to accepting occasional monetary gifts from men like Howard Simmons in exchange for information like this. A male, he answered, mid thirties, out on Pheasant Hill Road.

Simmons swirled his cocktail, a buzz of excitement building in his blood. Dead?

Not quite.

I see. Taking a sip of his drink, Simmons let the tension drag out, because sometimes the actual facts were such letdowns. And this unfortunate man has been . . . identified?

He certainly has, counselor.

As?

As one Colt Taylor.

Simmons smiled, relishing the news. Vengeance, Santiago style. The only question was what had taken so long.

The weapon?

Broken glass was discovered at the scene. It appears the weapon was a beer bottle.

Of course, Simmons thought, what else?

And the severity of the wounds?

About what you'd expect, Pursley drawled, from a broken beer bottle.

Simmons set his drink down on the patio table and gazed out at the harbor lights glittering in the dark while Captain Pursley, in a lethargic rattle of a voice exacerbated by forty years of smoking, filled him in on the details. Following up on an anonymous phone tip from a male with a decidedly Hispanic accent, a patrolman named Kershaw had discovered the unconscious victim lying in the middle of Pheasant Hill Road bleeding from a dozen different wounds, mostly facial. Unable to staunch the flow of blood, Kershaw had called an ambulance, which transported the victim to the Panama City hospital, the closest emergency room open that late.

With his free hand Simmons scribbled a series of notes on a yellow legal pad, anticipating Teddy Mink's eventual questions. The name of the patrolman called out to the scene, the nature of the wounds, the alleged weapon. With a smug look of satisfaction—brazen violence, after all, trumped the hell out of tax evasion—Simmons topped his drink off with another splash of vodka. Ever since the incident at the Black Kat Club three weeks ago he had been anticipating Jimmy Santiago's revenge, a bet he would have laid odds on, and now won. For if there was one thing the lawyer had learned in his twenty-odd years of criminal practice, it was that no one ever forgot, or forgave, a wrong.

I want to thank you for calling, Captain. It's always a pleasure, even under circumstances as dire as this, to hear from you.

My pleasure, counselor.

Hanging up the phone, Simmons consulted his directory and dialed Maggie Paterson's number, the second time he had called the poor woman in the last three weeks. Not that she would be, he supposed, particularly surprised to hear what he had to tell her. You lie down with dogs you wake up with fleas. He shook his head at the vagaries of the human heart. Such a bright and engaging young woman; why choose a loser?

At the Panama City emergency room a doctor informed a distraught and exhausted Maggie that Colt's numerous wounds had required a staggering forty two stitches to close. There were also, the doctor continued, referring to the patient's chart, at least three broken ribs as well as a nasty contusion in the lower back caused, he speculated, by the toe of a boot.

The next morning, following a final examination by the attending physician and an abrupt, inconsequential interview with a local detective who had already been instructed by Captain Pursley to close the book on the case as quickly and quietly as possible, the patient was released into Maggie's care. In the hospital parking lot, she helped him climb into the passenger seat of her jeep, waiting until he maneuvered his throbbing body into a tolerable position before turning over the engine and easing out of the lot, joining the flow of traffic on Bonita Drive.

Thanks to Raul's parting shot, a swift boot kick that caught Colt square in the jaw, it was painful to speak, and Maggie had to roll up her window to hear him.

Have you told Hunter yet?

Not yet.

Behind the puzzle of bandages that swathed most of his face, Colt mulled this over.

So where is he?

At Lureen's.

Okay. Colt grimaced as Maggie swerved to avoid a pothole. I guess that's okay.

Maggie tried, without success, to keep the strident note out of her voice. Okay? To tell you the truth, I don't see as I had much choice.

Colt lifted a rubbery hand to ward off her outburst. No no, of course not. Grimacing again, he tried to lean forward a few inches to ease the pressure on his ribs. I didn't mean it that way.

The first day back home, buzzed on painkillers, he never left his bed, allowing Maggie, as long as she was willing, to wait on him hand and foot. She called into work to request an extra day off, staring up at the ceiling as Cain the Pain offered his condolences for her troubles (which everyone in town had apparently already caught wind of) before assuring his "favorite cashier" that she could take as much time off as she needed because he, the Pain, was there for her, come hell or high water, darlin', come rain, snow or shine. Suppressing a derisive laugh— darlin'?—she redialed the phone, calling Lureen to confirm that Hunter was coming home on the bus after school and not stopping at his aunt's house to play with his cousin Toby. Then she gathered up a handful of root vegetables from their truck patch for a stockpot of soup, laid Colt's meds out in sequence on the kitchen counter and finally, re-entering the bedroom, reminded the patient of the doctor's orders to drink, whether he wanted to or not, eight glasses of water per day.

After lunch she knelt down like a penitent on her hands and knees to scrub the kitchen's linoleum floor. It was imperative to stay busy and keep her worrisome thoughts at bay. On the drive over to the hospital in Panama City she had concluded, once and for all, that despite his most recent litany of promises Colt was never going to change, and that this was no longer acceptable. As the jeep sped down the empty highway she made up her mind. No more trips to emergency rooms or holding tanks, no more phone calls from Howard Simmons in the middle of the night. When Colt recovered from his injuries she would simply announce that it was time for him to leave. Cutting the man loose wasn't going to be easy, and yet what else could she could do now but take stock of her situation, admit her ghastly mistake, and start over?

She would stay in the cabin with Hunter, the only shelter

the boy had ever known. The rent was cheap, the landlord mostly absent, and while the idea of raising a child alone was more than a little daunting, the alternative, granting custody to the father, was unthinkable. She would allow Colt to see his son whenever he wanted to if he gave her sufficient prior notice and if in exchange he agreed to handle the separation like an adult, for Hunter's sake. When Colt and Maggie's paths happened to cross they would remain civil, putting up a brave front to ease the child's understandable distress. They might even agree to attend, side by side, certain benchmark events in Hunter's life: graduations, ballgames, school plays. But no matter what Colt said or did, Maggie would never let him weasel his way back into her good graces, which is precisely what, she was fairly certain, he would eventually try to do.

Hearing the school bus grind to a stop at the end of the driveway, she charged outside into the spotlight of the sun as the door wheezed open and the driver, unreadable behind his Ray-Bans, stared right through her without the courtesy of a gesture or a word. Ignoring the surly driver—what was *his* fucking deal?— Maggie leaned over and kissed Hunter on the cheek before looping an arm around his bony shoulders to usher him down the lane.

On the back lawn she wrestled off his backpack and set it on the grass. Listen, honey, there's something I have to tell you.

He looked up at her with those big brown eyes and she felt her resolve momentarily falter. It's your father, she finally said, your dad . . . She wasn't quite sure how to put this. How do you tell a six year old that his father's face has been cut open with broken glass?

He's been in a little accident.

The brown eyes grew wide but the voice remained small. What kind of an accident?

Maggie knelt down and squeezed both of his arms. She felt like a water pipe under immense pressure, surely about to burst. Remember how I told you that you have to be careful around strangers because there's some bad men out there who might try to do you harm?

Yeah?

Well one of those bad men attacked your father last night. And he beat him up pretty good.

She couldn't look at him, couldn't handle the sudden fear in the boy's eyes, so she stared over his shoulder at a sparrow hawk gliding over the treetops on a current of invisible air. Once, in a 747, she had pressed her face to the little oval window to gaze down, with something like love, at the beautiful, broken world . . .

Mama?

She was plummeting back to earth, falling through space. She squeezed the boy's arms again. Now don't you worry, honey, your dad's gonna be okay.

Hunter bit his lower lip to keep it from trembling. Are you sure?

Of course I'm sure! It's just gonna take awhile, 'kay?

A trace of a smile: brave, heartbreaking. 'Kay, he said.

They crept down the hall. Lost in a tangle of sheets Colt stirred when the light from the open doorway spilled across the bed. Gradually his puffy eyes focused on Hunter standing in the doorway as if awaiting permission to enter the room.

Hey, buddy. He patted the rumpled sheets. Come on over here. Don't be afraid.

Shocked by his father's resemblance to a mummy, Hunter looked up at his mother for confirmation before timidly crossing the room.

15

When Maggie arrived at the store, her father met her at the front entrance. On any other occasion Frank would have held her at arm's length, beaming with pleasure at this lovely creature he had somehow, in the throes of passion, helped create. Look at you, he would have said, little Maggie Paterson, the apple of her daddy's eye. But no such endearments were forthcoming today. Today Frank's brow was furrowed with concern, the lightheartedness that made him so attractive to even the most casual acquaintances nowhere in sight.

C'mon in, honey. Let's go back to the office. I made us some tea.

Maggie sipped from her Mason jar, cringing a bit at the tea's cloying sweetness. When she was a little girl she had craved this sugary concoction more than any other, pedaling home from the movies on a Saturday afternoon. But those halcyon days had faded into memory a long time ago, replaced by the world of adulthood, which as the years raced by became more and more incomprehensible. Among other things she had to worry about now, there was her figure. On the drive into town it had occurred to her that without Colt around she would soon be forced to negotiate her way through the minefield of available men again—adult dating!—an idea so preposterous she nudged it right out of her mind.

Even though she knew that Lureen had already painted the broad picture—a wanton attack by an unknown (wink wink) assailant out on Pheasant Hill Road—Maggie wanted to make sure Frank understood that no matter what happened to Colt from here on out, she and Hunter were not in harm's way.

Those people he hangs out with. Frank stared at the floor, unable, or unwilling, to finish.

I know, Daddy. Believe me, I know.

Teddy Mink. Jimmy what's his name, Santiago.

In lieu of a rejoinder, Maggie swallowed another gulp of tea while Frank continued to contemplate the floor, wringing his worried hands.

Lureen says he's gonna be okay. Frank looked up at her with bloodshot eyes. Is that true?

Maggie frowned at okay; words were so relative, and sometimes meant nothing at all. Well he won't look the same, that's for sure. But no, there's no permanent damage.

Coulda been worse you know.

Yeah, I know.

Coulda been dead. Frank hesitated again. Raising children had once seemed like such a gift, the world through his daughters' innocent eyes. What about you, honey? You okay, too?

She felt the sting of tears and turned away, pretending to study the new chifforobes out on the showroom floor: walnut veneers, beautifully book matched, from across the rolling sea. I'm fine, Dad, I'm just fine.

But she wasn't, really, and neither was he. So she went ahead and blurted out the big news, describing how, when she gave Colt his walking papers, he had obediently packed his suitcase and marched right out the door. As if he had been expecting this, she added, all along.

Unable to assimilate what Maggie had just told him, Frank waited a few seconds before forming his next question. He left?

Yep.

Just like that?

Just like that.

Her father was momentarily speechless, some essential part of his psyche still suspended in disbelief.

He didn't shout? He didn't scream?

Not a whimper.

And you don't think he'll come back? You don't think he'll get drunk some night and, you know . . .

Maggie reached over to pat her father's knee. Look, I know it's been hard for you ever since Colt and I got together, for you and Mom both. I know you never approved of him, and believe me, I understand why. But for all his faults he never raised a hand to me, Dad, or to Hunter either. Not once. He hits *guys*. He hits *drunks*. When they get out of hand, he hits his friends.

What he's paid for, Frank gasped.

That's right. Because he lives in this . . . netherworld, Teddy Mink's world. And it's changed him, Dad. It's turned him into someone I don't even recognize anymore.

Frank nodded in commiseration. Well I know he loves that boy. I do know *that* much.

As their conversation faded into silence Maggie heard, from the back room, the unmistakable whine of an orbital sander. She looked over at her father, who was staring into the middle distance, imagining life without Colt Taylor after all. It was like imagining a vacation, a long road winding through the heart of some cool, misty mountains. The clouds broke open to reveal a snow-capped peak, and Frank's heart soared.

Is that a sander?

Sporting a beatific smile now, her father tilted his head at a funny angle, like a birder listening for the tweet of a distant junco. Yes, dear, I believe it is.

But I thought Cory took a powder.

He did.

Then who's running the sander?

Frank shrugged, so relaxed now he thought he might crumple to the floor and just lay there awhile, daydreaming. Colt Taylor, banished! Dieter, he murmured. That would be Dieter.

Who?

Dieter!

Who the hell's Dieter?

Suddenly energized, Frank hopped to his feet, reached out a fleshy paw, and lifted Maggie out of her chair. C'mon, honey, I wanna show you something. You're not gonna believe this.

With a sweep of his hand Frank presented the tea cart Dieter had refinished the previous week, prominently displayed now next to the front window. The cart's mahogany veneer, formerly curled and chipped beyond repair, or so Frank had assumed, now lay flat as a bed sheet, crowning a cluster of legs. The water stains that once marred the top had miraculously vanished. And the new satin finish—*five* coats of lacquer, Frank crowed—gave the cart the kind of patina collectors treasured.

Stunned by the transformation of this once-forgettable object that had moldered for years in a far corner of the showroom into something that might look at home in Buckingham Palace, Maggie could only mouth one long Wow.

This Dieter, he did that?

He certainly did, Frank replied. Guy's a craftsman, old school.

Maggie ran a hand across the top of the cart, which was smooth as stainless steel. She was genuinely impressed by the handiwork, and yet at the same time a troubling thought took root. It's beautiful, Dad, but . . .

But what?

Well look, I know business has been a little slow.

And?

And work like this—she nodded at the tea cart—must be pretty pricey, right? What I mean is, can you really afford this guy?

In a spasm of joy Frank flung an arm around Maggie's

shoulder and gave her a mighty squeeze. Well that's the beauty of it, honey. Dieter works for free!

As Maggie was struggling to cope with this bizarre and unsettling revelation, Dieter strolled out of the back room, wiping his hands on a shop rag. He caught sight of the woman standing next to the front counter and immediately recognized her from the photograph Frank had shown him a couple weeks before. Maggie, the first born. With that tangle of curly red hair framing her cameo-like face, she reminded him of a young Colleen Dewhurst strolling down the sidewalks of Seattle with the Duke himself in *McQ*. Speaking of the devil, Frank gushed, here he is! C'mere, boy, I wancha to meet someone!

Stunned beyond speech, unable to croak out even a simple hello, Maggie offered the gorgeous young man she had last seen swimming naked across her pond her limp, tentative hand.

16

On sweltering summer days like this one Hunter liked to go over to Aunt Lureen's house because his cousin Toby had an awesome swimming pool and a killer swing set and a mother who whipped up batches of goodies for them to munch on to their hearts' content, chocolate chip cookies and pb&j sandwiches and sometimes, on special occasions, banana splits. So when Maggie shook him awake on Saturday morning, the first weekend since Colt had left, and asked him what he would like to do today, he didn't hesitate.

Go to Lureen's! Please, Mama, can we go to Aunt Lureen's?

Of course, Lureen said on the phone. Why don't we make it a slumber party? I'll grill up some burgers and the boys can eat outside.

Thanks. I'm sure they'd like that.

To prevent Toby, who was sitting at the kitchen table shoveling away at a bowl of Rice Krispies, from overhearing her, Lureen lowered her voice. The way I figure it, Mag, after what you've been through? You could probably use a little time alone.

Or with some absolute hunk of a man, a stallion, Maggie

thought wildly. Ridin' tall in that saddle again! On her way to Hunter's bedroom she caught a glimpse of her reflection in the hallway mirror and wondered not for the first time in recent days just who in the world this hussy was. Lately she had fallen under the spell of a series of elaborate fantasies and erotic dreams, like the one last night featuring her and Dieter swimming buck naked in the warm, shallow waters of the pond. In her five years with Colt she had not strayed once, not once, but now that he was gone something in her libido had broken loose, a live wire carrying enough voltage to light up an entire town. In idle moments she felt ashamed of herself even though she hadn't done, strictly speaking, anything at all. She was almost thirty. It was an itchy age.

While the kids splashed around in the pool, Maggie and Lureen kicked back on the patio with Virgin Marys topped by stalks of fresh celery, the leaves still on.

You remember that church at St. Teresa's, Mag, the one we used to go to when were kids?

St. Teresa's? Sure, I remember it.

Well the funniest thing, I've been dreaming about that old church for two or three nights in a row now, those stained glass windows and that altar rack with all the votive candles. We each lit one when Grammy died, remember?

Maggie flushed, feeling soiled. Little sister dreaming about chapels while I imagine men in black leather chaps spreading my legs open in the shadows of their phallic Harleys. What did it all mean? Fortunately Lureen's husband Charley chose that moment to come home, to burst through the patio door and derail Maggie's dark train of thought by giving her such a spirited hug she feared her spine might crack. Good old Charley, a hugger and a hand shaker, a hale and hearty fellow born with a silver spoon in his mouth, and damn grateful for it, too. So what if he wasn't the brightest bulb in the chandelier? Sometimes it was better to be pure of heart, Maggie decided, than keen of outlook. Besides, as long as Charley kept his nose clean he would inherit his father's newspaper anyway, and little sister wouldn't have to work another day for the rest of her strange, enchanted life.

You look like a million bucks, Mag. Charley's voice was a megaphone, his enthusiasm charmingly boyish, his eyes like tiny black pearls buried in the fleshy folds of his face. He was tall and broad-shouldered and gregarious, but he bored easily too, and girl talk was basically incomprehensible to a man like him. After lingering for awhile on the patio, hooting at the kids in the pool, he executed a clean escape. Almost immediately the television in the study rattled on and Lureen smiled apologetically at her sister to indicate her love for the big clod, warts and all.

And why not, Maggie thought with a twinge of envy. Why shouldn't she love her man? He didn't cut up his friends with beer bottles or mule dope down to Islamorada or kowtow to criminals like Teddy Mink. He went to work in the morning and came home at night and tucked his child into bed. Life, after all, was a series of compromises, and when you came right down to it Lureen, by embracing those compromises, had done just fine. In sisterly accord Maggie lifted her Bloody Mary to Lureen's good fortune just as Charley turned the volume up on the mechanical laughter of a crowd of rubes in L fuckin' A responding, without a trace of spontaneity, to the guy with the cue cards.

So it didn't take him long, huh?

Maggie stirred her drink with the celery stalk. Didn't take who long?

Colt.

Maggie hesitated, eyeing her sister sideways. I don't know what you're talking about, Lureen. And I'm not sure I wanna know.

Shacking up that way.

Shacking up what way?

With Nicky Meyers!

It was as if little sister had pulled the latch securing the trap door. Maggie dropped seven excruciating feet; then the noose snapped.

Nicky Meyers? The stripper? Are you kidding me?

You mean you hadn't heard?

I hadn't heard!

Later Lureen suggested yet another upcoming church function—some kind of barn dance this time, replete with bales of alfalfa—but Maggie blew her off. She pictured a pod of Christian hayseeds circling around her quoting passage after passage from the Book of Whatever. I'll think about it, she said, meaning, no. Say goodbye to Charley for me. And thanks for watching the boys.

She gave Toby and Hunter a departing wave, deciding on her way out that Lureen was right, a quiet night alone would do her battered spirit a world of good. She'd stop at that new Cajun sandwich shop and pick up a muffaletta positively oozing with garlicky oil. Toss back a couple glasses of Chardonnay out on the dock to take the edge off, then a puff or two of weed. What harm would a couple tokes do? Comfortably numb, she'd watch perch nip mayflies while the moon, that trusty old balloon, rose over the white cedars. And wasn't there an old Hitchcock on the tube tonight, *Marnie*, maybe, or *The Birds*?

But as she was pulling out of Lureen's driveway Maggie noticed, to her dismay, none other than Dieter strolling down the opposite sidewalk, and her plans abruptly changed. On an impulse she began to tail him, to stalk him, driving slowly through the town's elegant Victorian neighborhoods, pausing every few minutes to let her quarry surge ahead.

Ten minutes later, when Dieter finally circled back to the town square, Maggie swung into a parking space right behind him and tooted her horn. At the sight of her, Dieter's face lit up.

Maggie!

Don't let him fool you, her inner voice cautioned. Don't let him charm you the way he apparently charmed Dad. Remember why you're here.

Hey, Dieter.

Hey.

Maggie climbed out of her jeep, realizing that it was too late to turn around now and drive back home. Listen, I'm sorry to bother you like this but I think you and I need to talk.

Sure. Here? An outstretched hand indicated the plaza. Right here?

Right here.

Fine. So what's on your mind, Maggie?

She glanced across the plaza. Near the junction of the two walkways that crisscrossed the center of the square, Uncle Billy was down on his knees digging up a flowerbed with a hand spade. Next to him was a tray of miniature roses.

What's on my mind, Dieter, is my dad. It was a flat, emotionless statement Maggie hoped would elicit some kind of knee-jerk reaction, something to confirm her suspicion that Dieter had an ulterior motive for befriending Frank. But her quarry remained silent, assuming a zen-like calm.

Unable to decipher this lack of response, Maggie stumbled on. Look, I don't know anything about you, okay? Where you're from or why you're here, in Crooked River. And I don't wanna know. It's none of my business. But my dad, well . . . my dad *is* my business.

Another uneasy silence, Dieter waiting, Maggie's nerves lit . . . Look, man—

You wanna know what my angle is?

This bald, abrupt statement so emboldened her she couldn't keep the sneer out of her voice. Well that's one way of putting it.

Overhead a noonday sun was burning a hole in the sky. If they were going to talk, Dieter suggested, they had better get out of this heat. He pointed to a nearby bench in the shade of one of the red oaks. Where they sat side by side with enough space between them to maintain the emotional distance Maggie's combative attitude had already established. Dieter folded his hands in his lap and Maggie felt a sudden surge of pity for the man. I don't mean to get up in your face like this, she said, but I'm confused.

About what?

Like he didn't know? Once again Maggie's suspicion overwhelmed her halfhearted attempt at civility. In her mind she saw her dad standing next to the new chifforobes with that goofy grin on his face. *That's the beauty of it, honey, Dieter works for free!*

Can we cut to the chase here, Dieter? Can we skip the bull?

He lifted his hands palms up and said Fine, not intimidated, as far as Maggie could determine, though certainly leery. He would be a hard man to trap—too careful, too watchful—so she went ahead and laid her cards on the table instead. Why dick around? No one, she announced gravely, staring at the side of his face, works for free. Okay?

He turned toward her with a look, if she wasn't mistaken, of bemusement. Oh, that.

Yeah, that.

They each took a breath, like two boxers retiring to their respective corners at the end of the first round. Across the plaza Uncle Billy placed one of the miniature roses in the small cavity he had just dug. Meanwhile Dieter stole a shy glance at her and she noticed that his eyes were the palest blue, the sky at sunrise, or the harbor in the middle of the day.

I met your dad one night by accident, out in front of his store. We got to talking and we hit it off, that's all. I like the guy. I like to listen to his stories.

Maggie had the impression that it wasn't easy for Dieter to open up, that he was basically a listener, an observer, ego free. Which meant in bed (which she tried, in vain, not to imagine) he would be attentive, generous, precise. She tempered her tone.

So you offered to do some work for him.

That's right.

For free.

A small, crooked smile. Well, not exactly free.

Maggie gathered her thoughts, thrown off balance again. Dieter might have been amused by these stabs at friendly banter but her emotions were as tangled as a briar patch, suspicion, irritability, and raw physical attraction all rolled into one.

Moreover, she'd forgotten how to flirt.

Not exactly free? What's *that* supposed to mean?

He buys my lunch.

Your *lunch?*

When I work, he buys my lunch.

And that's when you listen to his stories.

Exactly.

She wasn't about to give in this easily. Yeah, well, lunch isn't much of a paycheck, is it.

Hey, those are some pretty darn good lunches!

She had to admit that this side of him—his mischief—was terribly attractive. And his explanation was just bizarre enough to be true. God knows her dad could tell some whoppers.

When Dieter, without warning, reached over and touched her hand—a slight pressure of fingertips against her knuckles— she almost jumped out of her skin. I understand your concern, he murmured, and his voice was as gentle as the breeze that soughed in the boughs of the oak they were sitting under. You're being protective. I admire that. For a time he was silent again, withdrawing his hand and staring across the plaza at Uncle Billy, who was spreading around the miniature roses rings of cedar mulch.

Let me tell you something, Maggie, when your dad talks about you . . .

For a blind moment she wanted him to touch her again, to rub her arm or pat her shoulder or lean over and whisper in her ear exactly what Frank had said.

When he talks about me what?

Dieter thought about it for awhile, measuring his response. When he talks about you there's a kind of . . . adoration in his voice.

The men Maggie knew didn't speak this way, didn't use words like *adoration.*

Love, she whispered.

Yes, love. Unconditional love.

Uncle Billy hobbled down the flower row. As long as Maggie could remember, the old gardener had been here, tending his beds. But one day he wouldn't be. One day she'd pick up the newspaper and see the poor man's ancient, weathered face on the obit page. Dieter was still talking but Maggie no longer registered his words. She was watching Uncle Billy on his knees again, planting miniature roses. The old gardener would die soon and in time Frank and Janice would too. And then all the rest of us, her and Dieter and Lureen and Charley and everyone else, even Hunter. One day in the not so distant future, every single person walking around the town square today would be nothing but dust, ashes and dust. It was intolerable.

Since this is bothering you so much, Dieter was saying, I think the best thing for me to do is march on over to the store and tell Frank I can't work there anymore. Tell him I better quit. Tell him I'm leaving town.

But you can't do that, Maggie practically shouted. The expression on her face when she whirled toward him was a summer storm: gusty wind, banging shutters, spitting rain. Her hair was the color of fire.

But I thought that's what . . . I mean I thought—

You thought what? That you'd just up and leave?

Well I thought—

Who'll have lunch with him then? Who'll listen to his stories when you're gone? No sir, I'm afraid you can't do that.

All of a sudden she felt delirious, crazed with joy, one step away from delirium. She flashed him a toothy smile.

Jesus, Dieter, a guy can't blow into town the way you have and then just leave, you know. What's the matter with you anyway?

17

You sure you're up for this, buddy?

Clutching his 3-wood like a cane, Colt twisted his torso in both directions. A twitch of pain in the damaged ribs but nothing he couldn't handle. What about all the old codgers who gimped around golf courses like this three or four days a week? How much pain were *they* in? *Good to go, Boss.*

Shaking his head in grudging admiration, Teddy Mink considered the first hole, a straightforward par four: trees on the right, a nest of bunkers guarding the green, and a shallow fork of Hopkins Creek snaking across the fairway a hundred yards in front of the tees. Visualizing his shot, Teddy addressed the ball, flexed his knees, and proceeded to swing his driver as hard as he possibly could, in direct defiance of everything his new golf instructor had been trying, to no avail, to teach him about tempo. Along with Colt, who suppressed his glee by cupping a hand over his mouth, he watched the ball, after a brief, unimpressive flight, land thirty yards left of the fairway in a thicket of wiry grass.

No worries about the old ribcage, Colt mused. *I could beat this fucker with a blindfold on.*

By the fifth hole Colt was up four even though Teddy had already improved his lie three times and taken a mulligan on the second hole when he duck-hooked his tee shot into the estuary that drained Hopkins Creek. On the other hand, this wasn't really about golf. There were ulterior motives at work here.

The vista from the seventh tee was certainly one of the more scenic on the course, a par three over a picturesque pond swept by the loose arms of a weeping willow, the postage-stamp green nestled between a pair of pot bunkers that wouldn't have looked out of place in Wales. As Colt was admiring the layout, Teddy sidled up next to him and the mule knew that this was the moment his lord and master had been targeting all along. Here it comes, he thought; whatever it is, here it comes.

I talked to Jimmy Santiago today.

Oh yeah? How's he doin'?

Better. Teddy squinted at the far green. Pretty much healed, in fact. Kinda like you.

Colt winced. *Pretty much healed? Kinda like me?* Easy for you to say, he thought bitterly. The truth of the matter was that he would never completely heal, and that the scars on his face would serve as a constant reminder of that awful night out on Pheasant Hill Road. At first, the disfigurement had caused him a great deal of remorse. Hours in front of a mirror contemplating those untidy rows of sutures camouflaging the tears in his skin from Raul's lightning jabs while worrying about the wound the broken beer bottle had ripped open on his left cheek, the one he still hadn't seen. And yet when the last bandage was finally removed, it wasn't as bad as he had expected, the gash already closed over and stapled shut, leaving a crooked but not necessarily repulsive two-inch scar on the side of his face. Nicky Meyers, who had accompanied him to the clinic, didn't even flinch, and their acrobatic lovemaking that very same evening gave him further incentive to accept his changed appearance. Thoroughly sated, Nicky had traced a lazy figure eight on Colt's bare chest. Chicks dig scars, she groaned. They get off on stuff like that.

Colt wasn't sure what Nicky meant by this and doubted whether she did either. He had begun to notice that the stripper had an annoying habit of spouting off the wall comments that drew, at best, a puzzled response. Then again, no one really expected strippers to be deep thinkers, and the way Colt figured it, if Nicky was a bit of an airhead she more than made up for it in bed, and afterwards too, like last night when she suggested to her new paramour that Maggie Paterson must have been crazy to let a guy like him go. Drowsily content (among other positive developments, his doctor had just refilled his prescription of Percodan), Colt had gazed up at the silent, spinning paddles of the ceiling fan in Nicky's bedroom and muttered, Damn right she is. Woman's crazy.

He stabbed his tee into the ground and stepped back, sensing that Teddy's little performance wasn't over quite yet.

So I asked Jimmy how he felt now, you know, about the troubles.

Yeah? Colt nodded, attempting nonchalance. And?

And he said as far as he was concerned the troubles were over.

With a swing so rhythmic Maggie once said it was like watching a man having sex, Colt clipped his Top Flite with a deadly seven-iron and held on to his pose until the ball sailed over the willowy pond and rolled to a stop ten feet below the pin. Bingo!

Nice shot, buddy. Teddy raised his hand for a high-five because he thought that's what golf studs like Colt expected him to do. Then, frowning in concentration, he stepped up to the tee and took yet another mighty swat at his ball only this time, somehow, he caught it clean, square to the target. With his mouth hanging open in disbelief, Teddy tracked the flight of the ball as it arced high over the water before landing, with a distant thump, inches from the pin.

Holy shit, Boss, you stiffed it!

Yowzah!

After Colt lipped out his putt, Teddy tapped in for a two and started back toward the cart, pretending the birdie was no big deal. As long, he said, as Colt agrees.

What's that?

Teddy speared the putter into his bag. What Jimmy said; as long as Colt agrees.

No shit. He said that?

His very words. Verbatim. Colt climbed into the cart. He wasn't sure what verbatim meant but the rest of it sounded pretty good. An eye for an eye? Why not? At this stage of the battle, his spat with Santiago was no longer significant. All that mattered was for Teddy to assume that his kingdom was intact.

Well, feel free to tell Jimmy that Colt certainly does agree, Boss.

Before disengaging the cart's handbrake, Teddy glanced over at his mule, unquestionably pleased. Now, see that? That is *exactly* what I told Jimmy you'd say. Of course Colt will agree! Why wouldn't he?

Playing out the string, Colt curled his fingers for a fist bump, knowing how much stock Teddy put in such meaningless macho gestures.

Thanks, Teddy, I appreciate this.

Forget about it!

No, I mean it. The way you handle these things, sometimes I don't know how you do it.

Graciously accepting the praise he so richly, in his mind, deserved, Teddy shed the persona of casual weekend golfer so he could assume the more endearing role of Godfather, one of his favorites. He stopped the cart to gaze out over the glistening fairways, as if waiting—in this, the movie of his life—for the violins to swell.

Let me tell you somethin', buddy. Over the course of a lifetime, a man's lucky if he has three or four real friends. True friends, genuine brothers. You know what I'm sayin' here?

I think I do, Boss.

What I'm sayin' is, a man never wants to lose those guys.

Suddenly Teddy reached over and grabbed Colt's wrist and for a moment the mule was afraid that his lord and master had somehow read his mind, had somehow ferreted out the act of vengeance he had so meticulously planned. But he was mistaken. Blood, Teddy breathed, in a mime of passion. You and Jimmy. To me that's what you boys are, blood.

Resisting an urge to laugh out loud at Teddy's blatant histrionics—*Blood?* Did he really say *blood?*—Colt hung his head in feigned reverence and lowered his voice until it was appropriately small; husky with emotion, but small. You too, Boss, you too.

Later, sipping a gin and tonic in the air-conditioned clubhouse, Teddy got down to business, detailing the plans for the next run south, and the one after that, the pickups, the routes, the name of Colt's contact in the Keys. When he was finished he leaned back and clasped his hands behind his head, feeling expansive again.

Water under the bridge, old buddy. What I told Jimmy this morning; water under the proverbial fucking bridge.

Colt raised his glass in agreement, his own happiness mirroring Teddy's, and for better reasons. He polished off the rest of the scotch, basking in the glow of his deception. Because everything was falling into place, just as he had planned. Soon the score would be even. Soon, revenge would be his.

18

Maggie lingered in the stacks, dreaming. She let her hand trail across a shelf of spines the way she let her hand trail through a school of parrotfish the first time she snorkeled the Florida reef with Mom and Dad. The same flora and fauna she discovered underwater reproduced here in a coffee-table volume of dazzling photos and poetic text. Lavender plumes waving their slender fingers, stingrays skimming the floors of the canyons, sea whips. In a picture taken from a helicopter hovering over Montego Bay, the water assumed a color nature would be hard put to replicate, the cobalt blue she had seen in the paintings of Vermeer. Pigment so intense it brought back the skies of childhood and the ocean, that first time, from the windows of a plane.

Still daydreaming, she rounded the corner of the aisle and caught the roving eye of Jackie Banks, who was ostensibly flipping through a Rolodex, but in truth scoping out the stacks for boys of indeterminate age, as well as a few grown men. They liked to cruise here in their horn-rim glasses and black wingtips, shuffling down the Astronomy aisle only to emerge moments later at 18th Century Russian Lit. Coy, playful, fabulous, the ones Jackie hadn't already slept with averting their eyes when he looked up at them with his world-weary smile. For Jackie Banks was a towering figure to the furtive gay denizens of this backwater southern town, a flamboyant and unapologetic swordsman who didn't give a damn who knew what his sexual inclinations were, or how often he engaged in them.

Sometimes Maggie saw the other ones in the library too, the edgy young Lotharios women swooned over even if there wasn't a chance, the bad boys with slick black hair swept back in the style of a decade ago, sporting T-shirts and blue jeans that left nothing to the imagination except what boys like that might actually do with such equipment. Projecting a defiant toughness and some of them not faking it either, like their hero Jackie Banks, who decided one day that he was sick and tired of being bullied by Crooked River's homophobes and signed up for Taekwondo.

Even sitting down at his desk, he was a man who projected ease in his own body, confidence in the once bulky frame now trimmed of its last ounce of fat.

Well if it isn't little Maggie Paterson. Right here in the living flesh.

Grinning, Maggie set her books down on Jackie's desk and leaned over to receive the usual peck on the cheek. Without attempting to hide her amusement, she fingered the bright paisley collar of his latest outrageous shirt.

Look at you.

Jackie puffed out his chest, lifted up his chin. So what, he wanted to know, did Maggie think?

She studied the shirt's intricate pattern, all those colorful, exuberant squiggles. I think, she whispered, it's you.

Why of course it is!

They had been friends since high school, where Jackie graduated one class ahead of her before leaving town to study library science at Florida State. Upon his return they had struck up their friendship anew, Maggie and the town's most notorious sexual outlaw flaunting their freedom from the old strictures by cruising the bars and beaches for likely prey. Downing shots of Southern Comfort with the boy toys who blew into town on their way to somewhere else, would-be studs who didn't know what to make of the brazen young man on the arm of the sexy redhead, of his cackle of a laugh and unabashed flirtatiousness. Not that Jackie particularly cared. Even as far back as high school he had never been bashful, much less ashamed, of his sexual orientation, flaunting his right to sleep with anyone he chose even as he suffered the taunts of his schoolmates, the shoves in the hallway, the yanked hair, the beatings out behind the bleachers. He suffered the taunts of intolerance right up until the night two toughs confronted him in the center of the town plaza, in the stern shadow of General Lee. Fresh from that evening's class in Taekwondo, Jackie had finally snapped. The two bullies still laughing, still razzing the town's most outrageous homosexual even as his hands and feet, befitting a future black belt, lashed out in half a dozen different directions at once, connecting each and every time until the two bullies lay prone and pummeled on the sidewalk, begging him to stop. Naturally the story spread like an oil spill and the following morning the legend of Jackie Banks, Crooked River's first militant gay, was born.

With a flush of pride, Maggie recalled strolling down Main Street on Jackie's sinewy arm when he returned home from college, fully aware that there were those who refused to be amused by her friend's fey demeanor, Colt among them. Because her ex was an unrepentant redneck—there was just no way of getting around that fact—the kind of narrow-minded bigot small southern towns bred like flies. Not that Colt's homophobia mattered any longer, because he was out of the picture now for good. Moreover, she was traveling light on her feet today, still high from her encounter with Dieter the other day in the town square. An arrow from Cupid's bow had pricked her skin, and if anyone could understand what that arrow felt like, it was Jackie Banks. She smoothed his collar back down, giving his shoulder a motherly squeeze.

After work today? You're coming with me.

I am, huh? Jackie leaned back in his chair, eyeing Maggie with his usual glint of mischief. And what, pray tell, did you have in mind?

Excessive drinking?

Ooo.

General debauchery?

Now we're talkin'.

Seriously, big boy, how about a cocktail after work.

You got it, babe. Jackie glanced up at the wall clock. Gimme twenty minutes. I'll meet you there. He reached over to check out her books, lingering over each selection. Let's see now. Monet at Giverny? Check. Pauline Kael's film criticism? Check. Ansel Adams? Very good! But no novel today? Not even that new Ripley?

Ach, I forgot. And it's almost closing time! As Maggie spun back toward the stacks Jackie reached out and grabbed her wrist. Hey, I've got an idea. How about one by a *local* scribe?

One what?

A novel, by a local. Someone residing right here in our bucolic, little burgh.

Maggie pondered this. A novelist in Crooked River?

Who writes, Jackie promised, like an angel. Sex and drugs, steamy evenings on a Yucatan beach, blotter acid split two ways. How's that grab you?

Maggie batted her eyes in mock innocence. Did you say steamy, sir?

I said steamy.

Well I don't know, Mr. Banks, sounds rather risqué.

Don't worry, dear, he said drolly, I think you can handle it. He handed over her library card. Now go. I'll be there soon, and I'll bring the book with me. And hey, don't forget.

Maggie turned around. Forget what?

To order me a daiquiri. Queers *like* drinks like that.

They do, huh.

You bet. With lots of fruit. And one of those little umbrellas!

You are *such* a queen.

Why thank you, my dear.

They sat along a wall of windows overlooking the pool at the Holiday Inn, the water empty today except for a family of four, the kids and their mother splashing away while the father, hidden behind black shades, relaxed in a lounge chair with a copy of the local newspaper and a cooler filled with beer. Seemingly oblivious to his frolicking family, the father scanned the sports page while Maggie gave him the usual once-over, expecting Jackie to do the same. But when she looked across the table her friend was staring not at the hunk in the lounge chair but at her.

Talk to me, hon. Tell Jackie all about it.

So she did. The night in the emergency room, the tortuous last days at the cabin with Colt hobbling restlessly around the dark rooms while Maggie anguished over her decision; and finally the denouement, the ultimatum she gave Colt followed by a quiet conversation with Hunter, who burst into tears as his father's car sped down the driveway spraying gravel.

Jackie waited for Maggie to finish, impressed by his friend's resolve. She didn't falter once, didn't pout, didn't shed a single tear. Classic Maggie Paterson, he thought, a born survivor. Shake off the dust, kiss that sorry phase of your life goodbye, and get on with it. Running out of breath, she held up her glass for a refill. More, please.

Yes ma'am.

As Jackie sauntered up to the bar, Maggie checked out the pool again, the kids flopping around like seals in the sparkling water, the father immersed in his newspaper, the mother looking a little exhausted but hanging in there all the same, tossing a beach ball to her youngest. Watching the mother, Maggie hurt. Because that could have been me, she thought. That should have been me. If only I hadn't made such lousy choices.

Then again, she reasoned, I'm only twenty nine, hardly too old for another shot at happiness. A picture of Dieter in the town plaza flashed through her mind, raising gooseflesh. She upended her empty glass and let the dregs drip onto her tongue—lime pulp, and a little sweet juice—and thought about Dieter again, wondering what it would feel like to kiss him, to hold him, to coax him into her bed.

Hey, I almost forgot. Jackie set their daiquiris down on the table and reached into his leather satchel and withdrew the book he had brought for her. Your novel.

Maggie glanced down at the cover, an impressionistic rendition of a harvest moon perched over a stretch of tropical beach. She registered the title—*Jaguar Moon*—then flipped the book over to scan the blurbs. A favorable comment from Norman Mailer; a snippet of a rave review from the Washington Post, which named it one of the best books of the year; and then the capper, no less an authority than John Updike proclaiming the novel "This generation's *The Sun Also Rises*". Maggie was impressed.

You've read this?

I have.

And?

And it's as good as they say, Jackie replied.

She flipped the book over again. *Jaguar Moon*. Then her gaze locked on to the author's name and she felt the air in the room shift. No, it couldn't be. There was just no way. Her hands felt numb as she opened the back cover. And there it was, the author's photograph. As she closed the book Maggie's eyes lost focus and the room began to sway.

Maggie? Alarmed, Jackie reached across the table, touching her hand. He thought about his sister, an epileptic, who blanked out like this moments before an episode. Maggie! You okay?

What? She blinked a few times, like a child trying to shake off a dream. What?

You look like you just saw a ghost, girl. The fuck's the matter with you? Abruptly she stood up, rocking the table with her leg and spilling Jackie's daiquiri.

I gotta go.

But we just got here!

I'm sorry, but there's somewhere I have to go.

Because Jackie was right; Maggie *had* seen a ghost. And his name was William Dieter.

19

She tossed the book down on Dieter's bed and started to pace, like a caged animal, back and forth across the room. To the washstand, to the window, and back to the bed again, her jaw clenched, her words bullets.

So you're gonna write about us, right? I mean that's what you're doing here in Crooked River, right, writing about us?

What are you talking about?

Buncha rubes. Buncha hicks. Bet you even got our accents down, our cute little drawls.

Good Lord, Maggie, these . . . notions of yours. Dieter clutched the arms of the chair he was sitting in, facing his executioner. Write about you? What gave you *that* idea?

Whatdya think gave me that idea? She stabbed a finger in the direction of the book. That did!

Well you're wrong, okay? Please, sit down, you're making me nervous. He stood up to offer her the chair, the only one in the room, but she ignored him.

I suppose it's all some kinda game to you. Big-shot writer blows into town, pretending to be someone else.

Now hold on.

But Maggie wasn't about to. She plunged ahead, all systems go. And what's with the name, anyway? Why do you want people to call you Dieter? You're William!

No, I'm Dieter. Ever since I was a kid everyone's called me Dieter, everyone but my dad.

Oh yeah? Pacing, stalking, to the bed, to the window, to the chair. So what's *he* call you?

Billy. He calls me Billy.

This didn't seem to help.

Great, here I am in a hotel room with some guy named Billy who calls himself Dieter who writes a famous novel then shows up in town and doesn't tell anyone who he is.

Dieter lifted his hands in exasperation. Ever since Maggie burst into his room, flinging around her outlandish accusations, the target of her wrath had been backpedalling. But that was about to stop.

I never lied. Not to you or to anyone else.

Please. What the hell's that? I never lied?

All I'm sayin'—

What I wanna know, Dieter—and now she finally stopped pacing long enough to turn and confront him—is what the fuck's going on here?

To Consuela, who was standing in the hallway with her left ear glued to the wall, Maggie's question reverberated in more ways than one. What the fuck *was* going on here? At long last the much anticipated lover finally shows up in the person of Maggie Paterson, who, instead of immediately hopping into bed with our intrepid hero—the way Consuela certainly would have—lashes out at him with a vehemence that shocked even a seasoned housekeeper who had heard her share of vicious arguments erupt behind the Gibson's closed doors. Redheads! She pressed her ear against the plaster, straining to hear the rest of Maggie's rant.

As far as the housekeeper could deduce from the muffled conversation on the other side of the wall, what had triggered

Maggie's fury was a book, a novel called *Jaguar Moon*. But why would she be angry about a novel? To Consuela it sounded like another dead end, another unsolvable mystery. Then she recalled the sheets of yellow paper filled with indecipherable handwriting Dieter sometimes left on his desk, and all at once the picture became clear. Maggie was mad because Dieter was a writer and he hadn't told anyone, including her. A writer, for Pete's sake, he was a famous writer! The housekeeper started to swoon, grabbing on to the door jamb to keep from falling. Wait till she told Mr. Gold!

After awhile the voices in room 24 grew quiet and the housekeeper scurried down the hallway and slipped into room 26, leaving the door open a crack so she could listen some more. As soon as Maggie left—*if* Maggie left—she would race downstairs to share the startling news with Mr. Gold. How thrilled, how astonished the manager would be to learn that not only had Maggie Paterson—yes, that Maggie Paterson—visited Mr. Dieter's room, she had also exposed him as a famous writer traveling incognito down here to little old Crooked River to do some kind of undercover research for his next book. Just think of it, Mr. Gold, a writer, a scribbler, a scribe!

This explained everything, all those books on his desk, all those notepads. The quiet hours he spent alone in his room, holed up. And the way he spaced out sometimes, staring off into the middle distance, as if at nothing at all. Writers were like that, she supposed, deep.

Consuela heard the door to room 24 swing open and two pairs of footsteps shuffle down the hallway toward the stairs. For after much coaxing, Maggie had finally agreed to accompany Dieter to Ochoas, the Tex-Mex restaurant where he sometimes met Raul and his friends.

Hoping to maintain the emotional equilibrium Maggie seemed to have finally reached in the wake of her earlier tantrum, Dieter calmly explained as they crossed the town plaza that he no longer wrote.

But why? Why would anyone stop writing?

Dieter shrugged. Ask Harper Lee.

The woman who wrote *To Kill A Mockingbird*?

Right.

She quit too?

Quit stung, but what else could you call it? More than anything Dieter wanted to be honest with her. He was tired of all the secrecy, tired of deflecting every personal question aimed his way. At last he was ready to talk, and he had found, he hoped, the right person to confide in. They passed through a modest residential neighborhood, the houses half the size of the ones adjoining the plaza, and stopped at a busy intersection. Across the street, muted lights glowed in the windows of Ochoas.

Look, I stopped writing because I lost heart, okay?

Maggie didn't know what Dieter meant by this, but she knew that he meant it.

Heart?

You know, heart, drive. I couldn't do it anymore. I didn't see the point.

Her voice was gentle now, but still probing. You mean you forgot how.

No, that's not it. Dieter smiled, to take the edge off his words. It's more like I forgot why.

I don't understand.

To tell you the truth, I don't either. But there it is.

They waited for a Chevy pickup with a faulty muffler to roar past them before crossing the street. His feelings about it, Dieter admitted, were unresolved. He described the notes he had been compiling for the last few weeks, like an athlete who quits a race but continues to do calisthenics on the sidelines just in case he changes his mind.

Raul's wife Marlena, a striking young woman with a long black braid cascading down the back of her white blouse, greeted them at the door. As the hostess of Ochoas, Marlena made it a point to personally welcome every customer, particularly the regulars.

Dieter! She gave him a quick hug then stepped back to admire, with approval, his companion.

Marlena, this is Maggie Paterson. Maggie, Marlena.

Marlena offered her hand. The pleasure, she promised, is all mine.

When they were seated Marlena offered the two guests their menus, vaguely troubled now. Despite her initial delight at seeing Dieter out on the town with a date, something about his companion bothered her, though she couldn't pinpoint what that something was. It wasn't her looks; Maggie's flame of red hair was quite dazzling, and she had soft, intelligent eyes. And it wasn't her behavior. She was not the type, Marlena concluded, to put on false airs. No, there was something else causing her concern. She crossed the room and returned with two glasses of water, staring surreptitiously at Dieter's partner. Then with a sinking heart it dawned on her that Maggie Paterson was the name of Colt Taylor's girlfriend, and all at once that awful night out on Pheasant Hill Road blazed through her mind. With an inward shudder she saw the broken beer bottle knife through the air and open Colt's left cheek. And once again she felt ashamed to have let Raul talk her into playing the role of stranded driver on that terrible evening.

When Dieter asked what the special was Marlena answered, in a soft, subdued voice, carnitas, with plantains. Satisfied, he closed his menu. Sold.

And for you?

I'll have the same, Maggie replied. And bring us a couple margaritas, will you?

According to the rumor mill, after the incident out on Pheasant Hill Road Maggie and Colt had split up and Marlena wondered now if the attack had caused the separation. Then again Colt Taylor, by any account, was not much of a catch; surely Maggie was better off without him, especially if, in the process, she had snagged Dieter. Walking over to the stainless steel counter that separated the dining room from the kitchen, Marlena glanced back at the two and all of a sudden she felt better about the entire affair. Wildly rationalizing her own complicity, she abruptly decided that Raul's brazen act of revenge had actually been a kind of matchmaking. After all, if it weren't for that admittedly unfortunate incident these two might never have gotten together. In a way, Raul had done Maggie a favor by cutting up her man. Brightening, Marlena sang out the order to the cook, who was laboring over the kitchen's smoky grill—*dos carnitas, compinche!*

Maggie looked down at Dieter's hands resting on the table, confirming his lack of a ring. Her heart thrummed with expectation, but still, she had to get a hold of herself; *that* particular subject could wait for another time. Right now she just wanted to enjoy his company, have a few drinks and eat her carnitas, whatever those were. And after that? Well after that, who knew?

Did you order the drinks yet?

Dieter laughed. You mean you don't remember?

Remember what?

The drinks! *You* ordered them.

Of course I did! She slid her scarf off her shoulders and gave it a little twirl before hanging it off the back of an adjoining chair. Because that, she concluded, is what Audrey Hepburn would do in a scene like this, she would act as breezy as Holly Golightly strolling down the streets of Manhattan at sunrise, the world at her feet.

What's a carnita, Dieter?

Carnitas? It's pork, shredded pork.

The dinner was superb, spicy shredded pork surrounded by a mound of rice, a pool of pinto beans, and sweet plantains fried to a light char in a pan of clarified butter. To top it off, the margaritas were the best Maggie had ever tasted. She held up her empty glass, still rimmed with a mustache of salt.

So I bet this is the way they make em in Mexico, huh?

Depends on what part of the country you're in.

Do you miss it?

Mexico? He thought about that for awhile. I do, sometimes. But you can't go back again, right? There was a hint of regret in his voice, and it saddened Maggie to hear it.

Thomas Wolfe.

What?

You Can't Go Home Again.

He seemed surprised. You've read that?

Uh-huh.

I didn't know you were a reader.

Maggie leaned over, exposing a little cleavage. She hadn't played a seductress in a very long time. Actually, Dieter, there's a lotta things you don't know about me, she purred.

Pleasantly tipsy, they bid goodnight to Marlena and headed back to the Gibson, taking the circular route along the harbor. Dieter showed her where he liked to sit on the seawall in the mornings and watch the boats.

So let's sit, she suggested. She patted the top of the wall.

Dusk. Along the docks of the marina gusts of wind rocked the keels of the trawlers. Farther out, on one of the sailboats anchored offshore, a young woman tanned bronze by the sun was brushing a coat of marine varnish onto a teak handrail.

Maggie was silent for a few minutes, enjoying the view. She pictured Dieter sitting here in the mornings watching the deckhands fit out their boats.

Can I ask you something?

Of course you can.

It's none of my business but I'm gonna ask anyway, okay?

Fine.

Just tell me it's none of my business, okay? If it's none of my business—

It's okay. Dieter placed a finger against her lips, and then removed it. Ask away.

She looked out at the moon's pale reflection trembling on the surface of the harbor. Jen. That's your wife's name, right?

Ever since Maggie threw the book on his bed he had been

expecting this. Yes, he answered quietly, my wife's name was Jen.

With a flush of excitement Maggie noted the past tense. *Was.* It confirmed what she had suspected all along, that Dieter was recovering from a nasty breakup. This explained his reticence, his refusal to open up. It was simple. He didn't want to be hurt again, and who could blame him? In a way, he was just like her.

I saw the what-do-you-call-it, in the book.

The dedication. I figured as much.

To Jen, Jen . . . You repeated her name. That was sweet.

When Dieter didn't respond, Maggie slowed down. She wasn't sure how far to go with this. Sometimes a guy on the rebound was so sensitive the slightest tremor could throw him off course. If she probed too deep, he might dance away. And yet she had to know, she just had to.

So what happened?

What happened?

To you and Jen.

From one of the boats came the sound of breaking glass, followed by a bark of unpleasant laughter. What happened, Dieter murmured, is she died.

It was as if he had suddenly struck Maggie with his fist, punching the wind out of her lungs. Good God, Dieter, I'm sorry. I'm so sorry. How . . . I mean how—

Did it happen? He shrugged; what else, in the face of such folly, could you do?

She was driving home from work one night in the rain, he said. A car swerved across the center line . . . It happens, I suppose, all the time.

He fell silent, grateful that Maggie had stopped talking; because there was nothing more, really, to say, nothing anyone could possibly say. He had already heard all the inconsequential words, all the tired old platitudes that never rang true. Even Ecclesiastes had failed. Blessed are those who grieve, for they shall be comforted. But when? When would the sharp blade of his grief dull into mere sorrow? After the funeral he had walked around for days in an emotional fog, unable to weep, like some kind of zombie. The first time he broke down was a week later, on the trail behind their house. He had hiked that trail with Jennifer so many times, all the way to the end, to the cave of the albino fish. Without warning, remembering those walks, he had begun to cry, and at first it had seemed like a blessing, a cleansing, his penance. Then he couldn't stop.

In the doorway of the Gibson, Maggie thanked him for the evening. Then she leaned over to kiss his cheek but at the last moment Dieter turned and their lips met, hungry, famished. When they finally broke apart he asked, in a choked voice, if she would come up to his room.

With every breath in her body that was exactly what she wanted to do. But it was too soon for that.

Not yet, she whispered. Soon, but not yet.

20

Ten miles south of Crooked River, Colt cruised past one of the county's original honey farms and thought about his father stacking bee boxes in the glare of a noonday sun. Jesse Taylor: cop, beekeeper, fisherman. Husband. Killer. Dad.

In the turbulent wake of the accidental shooting of Tina Johnson, Officer Taylor had considered his options for gainful employment. The stingy pension he'd managed to squeeze out of the police department before they let him go only replaced half of the salary he had been earning. To keep up with his house payments he would have to establish a second source of income, and he would have to do it soon. Relatively speaking he was still a young man, and he strongly believed that it behooved young men who had fallen on hard times, whatever the circumstances, to continue to support their families.

Although he possessed few marketable skills, Jesse had always been interested in honey production, having, as a boy, toiled on one of the local farms. So after a few weeks of serious soul searching—would he really be able to make a go of it?—he secured a loan from the bank, leased a modest plot of land, and set up his bee boxes.

Unfortunately, three other honey farms with deep community roots were already well established in the area, and the owners of those farms didn't take kindly to an interloper like Colt's dad. In response, they formulated a strategy to monopolize the market and lock Jesse out, effectively forcing the new business, by the end of its first year, to fold.

Following the failure of the honey farm, Jesse found work in commercial fishing, hiring out as a deck hand on a friend's shrimper. But shrimping, he soon discovered, was so physically demanding he began to fear that his body would break down. Demanding, draining, debilitating, the hardest work he had ever done. He would trudge home at night so worn out all he could do was grab a bottle of blended whiskey from the cupboard and sit on the front porch downing shot after shot until the soreness in his lower back and the stink of shrimp on his fingers disappeared in an alcoholic fog. When the bottle was empty he would go inside and eat the supper his wife had left out for him—the juices of the meat congealed now, the vegetables cold.

All his father had ever wanted to be was a cop, and as far as Colt could determine he had been a good one. Clean, dedicated, efficient. For fifteen years his record remained impeccable. And then one evening a call came in alerting the precinct to a potentially explosive situation at an alleged drug house on Mulberry Drive.

Jesse and his partner were the first to arrive on the scene. According to the dispatcher, a call from a neighbor had described a loud, vehement argument spilling out onto the sidewalk, onto the street. Shouted threats, a sudden fistfight and finally, according to the caller, gunshots. But when Jesse and his partner pulled up to the house on Mulberry Drive, all was quiet. They drew their guns and crept warily toward the front porch. Standing off to the side, Jesse rapped on the door, to no response. He signaled his partner to call backup. Then he announced that he was going in.

Later Jesse told a team of investigators, sent down from Tallahassee in the wake of the shooting, that it was so dark inside the house he could hardly see what he was doing.

But why'd you go inside in the first place, one of the investigators asked. Why didn't you wait for backup?

Because I heard a child in there, Jesse mumbled. And she was crying.

Eventually Officer Taylor was cleared of any official wrongdoing but from that day on the shooting haunted his dreams and his work began to suffer. Time after time a bedroom door swung open and a bare-chested black man appeared in a glaring wedge of light, brandishing a pistol. Pointing his own gun, Jesse ordered the suspect to drop his weapon but the man ignored him, raising his shaky hand, waving the barrel in the air. At that point, Jesse told the investigators, I had no choice but to protect myself. He squeezed off a shot and then watched in horror and incomprehension as the bullet shattered the skull of twelve-year-old Tina Johnson, who had been standing behind her father the moment he dove away. Night after night Jesse woke in a sweat, sometimes screaming. Shell shock, his captain informed the commissioner, shaking his head. To avoid any further public outcry, the commissioner recommended dismissal, and the department let Jesse go.

Just south of New Port Richey, Colt stopped for lunch at a roadside cafe. The key to a drug run was to not think about the duffel bag stuffed with six kilos of cocaine locked and hidden behind a false panel in the trunk of your car. The key was to embrace distraction, to concentrate on something else, like the statuesque legs of the waitress, for instance, who now sashayed down the old-fashioned stainless steel counter to take his order, a tall, shapely blonde in her mid thirties with a pleasant if not particularly memorable face. When she caught him looking, she didn't shy away.

What'll you have?

Whatever you recommend, darlin'.

She was chewing gum, but he wasn't going to hold that against her. What I recommend, she replied, returning his bold stare, is that you tell me what you want. Why don't we start with that?

Colt waited a few moments, savoring the repartee. Then he folded his paper menu and slipped it back into its metal holder. What I want—I mean, you know, right now—is a Reuben sandwich. As the waitress sauntered away he checked her out again, head to toe. Those legs were driving him crazy.

The diner was a dive and his Reuben sandwich was almost tasteless but Colt didn't care. Even though there was only one other customer at the counter the waitress kept passing back and forth behind it, filling the salt shakers or replacing the ketchup bottles, any excuse to give Colt another glance at those astonishing legs. Once she even bent over, instead of kneeling down, to grab a handful of coffee filters from a cardboard box in a cabinet near the floor, stretching her white skirt tight across her bum.

That Reuben okay?

He slid the empty plate away. Tell you the truth, I've had better.

She leaned over the counter, lowering her voice. Yeah well, who hasn't? Without asking if he wanted any more, she refilled his glass with water. Then she set his check down next to it. So you headin' down to the Glades or what?

Talk to no one, Teddy advised. Do what you want on the way back, but on the way down, talk to no one.

Just passin' through, he said as casually as he could.

The waitress studied him for another minute. Too bad.

Ain't it? He laid a ten on the counter, grinning. 'Course you never know when a guy like me'll be passin' through again.

That right?

Catch you later, darlin'.

You do that.

By the time he reached the turnoff to Everglades City the sun had dropped below telephone poles crowned with osprey nests, casting a rosy glow over the hardwood hammocks. There was little traffic today and a deadly silence hung over the coastal prairie, that vast sea of grass. A couple miles past the turnoff he veered south onto an unmarked road where his tires churned dry gravel, raising a cloud of white dust and startling a snowy egret nesting in the dark arms of a roadside mangrove. Spooked, the egret wheeled over the tidal flats that bordered the road as Colt rolled down his window, smelling the brine in the air, close to the saltwater now.

If he had been given a choice, he would have preferred to drive on down to Islamorada tonight and get this over with. But Teddy Mink didn't like his mules to tire, so he had secured a safe house outside Everglades City, a place where Colt could get something to eat and a good night's sleep before continuing on in the morning.

He pulled up to a tee in the road and hung another left. In the distance, he could see the blade of a white sail and farther out, the dark smudges of the Ten Thousand Islands. Then the gravel road turned into hard-packed dirt scarred by deep potholes he swerved to avoid, driving at a snail's pace.

After two or three more bone-jarring miles, a weathered clapboard house loomed into view at the end of a shaded driveway. He pulled into the drive and got out of the car, stretching his legs. The safe house was silent. In the patchy front yard a tire swing hung by one strand of its rope from the crooked limb of a mimosa.

On the veranda that wrapped around the house he noticed movement, a shadow. Then the screen door creaked open, framing a petite middle-aged woman wearing frayed denim shorts and a loose Indian blouse. The woman's skin was walnut brown from the sun but oddly unwrinkled from such exposure. She approached the car, unsmiling, severe.

You must be Colt.

Yes ma'am.

She gave him a look. Ma'am? Did you just call me ma'am?

Colt shrugged, suddenly weary from the long drive. Look, I don't even know you, lady. I was just being polite. What, he wondered, was this bitch's problem?

Uh-huh. All business now, the woman nodded at an outbuilding, a fishing cabin built on stilts over the flats. A rickety dock extended out from the cabin, the old cedar pilings scarred and pockmarked by a hundred years of storms.

You can sleep out there.

Ignoring the woman's brittle attitude, Colt's eyes swarmed over her body even though the look she gave him in return squelched any desire his scrutiny might have triggered. The message behind that look was clear; don't even think about it, pal.

There's beer in the cabin, she said, and sandwiches. I can wake you in the morning whenever you want.

That's okay, I don't need anyone to wake me, lady. I'm a big boy now.

The woman shrugged. Suit yourself. Teddy said you'd be leaving early. I'll have some coffee ready for the road.

Thanks, um . . . sorry, but I didn't catch your name.

Without bothering to reply the woman spun on her heels and headed back toward the house before hesitating halfway across the yard. Colt tensed, wondering what kind of grief he was in for now.

Look, I don't mean to be bitchy, she said, but I've had a rough day, okay? Even though the woman was trying, without much success, to soften her tone, Colt made her wait a moment before he nodded. And my name, is Pam, Pam Morgan.

Now this is more like it, Colt thought, a little civility.

And mine, ma'am, is Colt Taylor.

His wry emphasis on ma'am made Pam Morgan smile even though she didn't particularly want to.

Well why don't you get some rest, Colt. I'll see you in the mornin'.

As the sun tumbled behind the mangroves, darkening the flats, he sat out on the dock with his legs dangling over the water, sipping his second beer. Despite his determination to keep his emotions in check until the run was over, his inner demons—anxiety, paranoia, and dread—had returned, as they tended to whenever he was carrying. The drug runs were lucrative, especially compared to the wages he earned down at the club, but the fears they generated were not easily dismissed. He chugged the rest of his beer and opened another one, trying to cheer up. Tomorrow, he told himself, would be a better day. As soon as he unloaded the coke the tension of the run would vanish and he'd drive home clean, without a worry. If he was in the mood, he'd stop at that diner again in New Port Richey and find out if the waitress with the astonishing legs was more than just a tease. Gazing out over the shadowy flats he heard, once again, her parting volley when he hinted that he might return. *You do that* . . . Then the screen door of the safe house banged open, and when he looked across the yard he saw Pam Morgan standing under the mimosa. She had changed into a yellow shift and moccasins and her hair was wet from a shower, and neatly combed.

The cabin okay?

It's fine.

Got everything you need?

Colt saluted her question with his beer bottle. All the comforts of home.

Frowning, conflicted, Pam scuffed the dust with one of her moccasins. Listen, Colt, about earlier . . .

Don't worry about it. He held up a hand. Believe me, I know how it is.

You do, huh?

Sure I do. Sometimes it comes down so hard you need a hat, right?

Pam grinned, genuinely amused this time. You got that right, a big old hat. One of those sombreros.

Colt considered the woman in the yard with new eyes. Now that she had lost her crappy attitude Pam Morgan was, if somewhat weathered, rather fetching. Rode hard and put up wet but not bad, he thought, not bad at all. He wondered how she had ended up here, in the middle of nowhere? Was she one of Teddy's ex-girlfriends, banished to the boonies, embittered and alone?

Anything I can do to help?

For a few moments Pam seemed to actually consider his question, its double entendre. Then she laughed. Well, I reckon not. But thanks for asking.

The next day he crossed the bridge to Islamorada around noon. The sun was high in the sky, its fierce light glancing off the bonefish boats anchored in the marina. Just past the marina he turned into a gravel lane that wound back through a copse of palms. At the end of the lane he saw the former dive shop Teddy had described to him. Knee-high weeds growing wild around the perimeter of the abandoned building camouflaged a For Sale sign stabbed into the ground: Harmon Properties.

He slid out of the car and leaned against the chassis, waiting for the buyer to arrive. The shade helped temper the intense noon heat but there was no breeze here and the air was thick with mosquitoes.

A few minutes later a cherry-red Oldsmobile nosed up the drive and parked behind Colt's rental. Wheezing from the effort, a large, florid man uncoiled his flabby body from the driver's seat and offered Colt a beefy hand. Harmon, he said.

Dieter, Colt thought. And now Harmon. The fuck happened to first names? Taylor, Colt Taylor.

Well grab your stuff, Colt Taylor, and come on in.

Sure thing, um . . .

Dub. Harmon opened his mouth in amusement, exposing a row of perfect teeth. The name's D.B. but you can call me Dub. Everyone does.

Sure thing, Dub.

Once inside, Colt took note of the front counter that ran the length of the room. Behind the counter a few dive posters were still tacked to the wall; otherwise the shop was empty.

Colt set the duffel bag on the top of the counter and stepped away, careful not to take his eyes off the realtor. He had muled dope down to the Keys a dozen times before, but Dub Harmon was a new customer, and with anyone new you had to be careful.

The realtor pointed at the duffel. You mind?

No sir.

As the big man unzipped the bag, Colt's gaze flitted out the window. His nerves were shot. On every run this was the worst time, the actual exchange. His fear bubbled to the surface, making his palms sweat. What if a curious cop happened to cruise down the lane and see their cars and step inside to investigate? Where would they hide the duffel? Six kilos. Enough weight to lock you away for good. Colt had an inordinate fear of prison. With his movie star face and well toned body he knew he'd be an easy target for every pervert lurking like a phantom behind those iron bars. He'd heard the horror stories, and they'd made him cringe.

He refocused on Harmon, who had opened the duffel and was examining the contents now, taking his sweet time. This—the realtor's laid back, unhurried manner—was exactly why Colt didn't like dealing with people he didn't know. Too many things could go wrong. What if Harmon had been tailed? Or what if, God forbid, he was undercover?

This last suspicion, paranoid or not, was particularly nerve wracking. He reminded himself that this was nothing more or less than a simple business transaction. Deals like this went down every day. Besides, Teddy Mink might be a grade-A prick but he was too smart for a setup. In all the years Colt had known him, Teddy hadn't been burned once, and he wasn't going to be now. For one thing, on this particular run, the real danger—a ripoff— had already been taken out of the equation when Harmon transferred the payment into Teddy's offshore account a week before Colt left town. All he was this time, Teddy had assured his mule, was a courier. But Colt's mind remained uneasy. Why, if the deal was so cut and dry, was the big man dicking around in that duffel? Why didn't he hurry the fuck up?

At last the realtor zipped up the duffel and led Colt back outside. He opened the trunk of the Oldsmobile and hoisted the bag inside and turned back around, offering his glad hand again. Pleasure to meetcha, Colt.

You too, Dub.

Harmon took a handkerchief out of his pants pocket and wiped his sweaty face. Even though the transaction was over, he didn't seem ready to leave just yet.

So let me ask you somethin', friend.

Wary again, Colt gave the realtor an almost imperceptible nod. He thought about the .45 locked in the glove compartment of his car. What good, he wondered, would it do if Teddy was wrong, if Harmon was about to double cross him?

You like the Keys, do ya?

The big man's breezy attitude was infuriating. Why didn't they just leave now, go ahead and part ways? Colt's paranoia reared its ugly head again. A double cross wasn't likely but what about a bust? He pictured half a dozen black-and-whites blocking the end of the lane, patrolmen with pointed guns, bullhorns.

Love 'em, Dub. Come down here every chance I get.

Harmon was sweating bullets but it didn't seem to bother him. He swiped his face again with the handkerchief. Well let me tell you something, son. You ever wanna move down here you gimme a call. Cuz I got places for sale all over these fuckin' islands!

I'll do that, Mr. Harmon. I'll keep that in mind.

Dub, son, call me Dub.

Five minutes later Colt was heading north again, breathing free and easy now, the knee-buckling stress of the exchange blown away by the sea wind streaming through the open windows of his car.

One more run, he thought, and I'll be done with all this. No more Dub Harmons, no more Teddy Minks. No more mule. In two weeks he'd drive back down to the Keys carrying more weight. Except this time he wouldn't make it. Because Eddie Tannenbaum would be waiting for him in Sarasota. Good old Eddie T., his former high school teammate who, like Colt, was going to turn those next six kilos of coke into a future of such ease and comfort it would make Teddy Mink's current lifestyle seem like a grind. Colt laughed, visualizing Teddy's face when he realized what had just happened. Hit 'em where it hurts, his father once counseled his son the night before a football game. Make 'em pay for it.

When he walked into the diner, the waitress practically melted. After another lively round of flirtatious banter—accompanied by another lousy sandwich, chicken salad this time—he slipped her a scrap of paper with his room number at the Rodeway Inn. Then he rose from his stool, shooting his cuffs.

So where's a guy get a stiff drink around here, darlin'?

The waitress glanced back toward the kitchen to make sure the cook wasn't eavesdropping. The Friendly Tavern, she whispered.

The one next to my motel?

That one. I'll be there in a jiff.

After so many rounds of Pina Coladas he finally lost count, Colt took the waitress back to his room where, following the third go round, she finally fell asleep. He counted his blessings. He was exhausted—the woman was an animal—and sore. On top of that, he was still so pleasantly drunk all he wanted to do now was lie back and picture his pad on the beach in that village south of Puerto Vallarta Eddie Tannenbaum, with his gift for gab, had so lovingly described. A Mexican villa with all the bells and whistles overlooking the turquoise sea. Palm trees rattling in the wind. Sailboats skimming the horizon. Cold beer, hot Latin ladies, tons of cheap grub. He imagined lying in a lounge chair with a cold Corona in his hand. In the distance, he heard the child's manic laughter followed by the mom's. Slipping on his shades, he saw Maggie and Hunter running down the beach waving their arms and calling out his name . . . As he woke, hungover, in his room at the Rodeway Inn, the waitress lay sprawled across the bed sheets, a thread of drool hanging from her lower lip. Looking at that fan of blonde hair (with dark roots, he now noticed) Colt felt a pang of guilt even though he knew it was unwarranted. Maggie, after all, was the one who had demanded, in no uncertain terms, that he leave. What did she expect him to be now, a celibate?

But no worries, he mused, because both of their lives were about to change and soon enough the breakup would be all but forgotten. For how could Miss Maggie Paterson, or any other woman for that matter, resist the scenario he was about to lay out for her? The villa he was going to purchase—complete with local housekeeper—for fifteen grand. The little town with its quaint Catholic chapel right next door to an open air cantina where you could kick back with an a cold drink and watch the surfers ride the waves. There were other expatriates living in the village, he'd tell her, a whole boatload. And my buddy Eddie from Sarasota, he'll be there too. Good old Eddie T., who had assured Colt that the school Hunter would attend was excellent, that the teachers all spoke perfect English, and that most of Hunter's schoolmates would be as American as apple pie.

Just think about it, hon. While Hunter's in school we can cruise out to one of the nearby islands for a picnic, or swim in the ocean, or just chill out on our own lanai. We can learn how to cook Mex, maybe grow some of those hot peppers you like so much. And on weekends we can drive down the coast and check out the cliff divers at Acapulco, wouldn't Hunter love that? Best of all, we won't have to work another stinking day for the rest of our lives. No more Winn Dixies, no more drug runs, no more Teddy Mink. Colt smiled in the dark, convinced that at long last his ship was about to come in and that Maggie Paterson would be standing on its bow waiting for him. Moonlight swims, margaritas on the beach, hot sex beneath the palm trees of Old Mexico; how could any woman in her right mind say no to all that?

THREE

21

The day after Consuela disclosed the startling news that the true identity of the Gibson's most intriguing guest had at last been revealed—that William Dieter was, in fact, a novelist of some note—Mr. Gold phoned a former schoolmate, the retired English professor Wilbur Meeks, to inquire whether his old friend had ever heard of the young writer, or possibly read his book.

Both, Meeks replied. Heard of him *and* read his book.

Which I understand—and correct me if I'm wrong, Wilbur—is held in high esteem by any number of critics?

Oh yes, Meeks confirmed, by critics and readers alike. It's quite a success, particularly for a first novel.

When Meeks asked Mr. Gold if he planned to read William Dieter's book, the manager admitted that the thought had, indeed, crossed his mind.

After a pause, the professor returned to the line, carefully choosing his words, as if he were about to broach a particularly delicate subject. I must tell you, Henry, that I'm a bit surprised at your interest in this particular . . . work.

But why, Wilbur, why surprised?

Meeks took more time to consider his response, determined to remain diplomatic. Because *Jaguar Moon*, he finally said, is a rather, well, graphic novel, sexually speaking that is. If you'll forgive my saying so, it just doesn't seem like your usual cup of tea.

Mr. Gold, who had previously confessed to professor Meeks that his idea of a good read was one of the swashbuckling tales of Mr. Alexander Dumas, did not take offense. When it came to matters of literary taste he was more than happy to defer to his learned friend. After all, Mr. Gold would later inform Consuela, a man does not gain tenure for twenty years at a prestigious state university without sterling—no, make that impeccable— credentials in his chosen field. Besides, the revelation that William Dieter was a modernist saved Mr. Gold the invaluable chunk of time he would have wasted slogging through *Jaguar Moon*. Because a man like me, he assured professor Meeks, gives little credence to these brash young Turks apparently intent on proving that decorum within the pages of a book is obsolete. Not that he had, mind you, ever actually read one of their books.

An amused Wilbur Meeks assured his old friend that he understood his position.

As you will no doubt recall, Wilbur, I was a happily married man for thirty five years. Right up until the day my dear Virginia, rest her soul, passed like an angel into the arms of the Lord. So I hardly need someone like young Mr. Dieter to describe, *ad infinitum* I suspect, the physical act of love. Some things, I dare say, are better left to the imagination!

Professor Meeks, who was thinking well there goes D.H. Lawrence, nonetheless reiterated his sympathy for Mr. Gold's opinion.

Thank you, sir. And now that we have *that* particular issue out of the way, may I let you in on a little secret?

Of course, Henry. Over the years Meeks had been privy to any number of Mr. Gold's "little secrets" and often found them pleasantly diverting.

To tell you the truth, Wilbur, the only reason I was even

remotely interested in *Jaguar Moon* is because the author happens to be staying with us here at the Gibson.

You're kidding?

Oh no, I'm not. For the last four weeks Mr. William Dieter has been residing right here in our humble abode. And I must say that over that period of time I have grown quite fond of the young man, quite fond.

Another pause, then Wilbur Meeks came back on the line, his voice subdued now. Such a tragic story.

Jaguar Moon?

No no, the real story, William Dieter's story.

When Mr. Gold confessed that he didn't know what his friend was talking about, Professor Meeks proceeded to fill him in on certain biographical details he had culled from a recent article in Esquire. How Dieter had met the love of his life, a young woman named Jennifer Rawls, down in the backwater Mexican village where he was writing his book. How upon completion of that book he had returned with Jennifer to his hometown in Indiana, where they were promptly married. And finally how those two admirable young lovers discovered, in this troubled old world of ours, both romance and success. For upon its publication *Jaguar Moon* was greeted by immediate and unqualified critical acclaim, a rarity for first novels.

And then a few months later, Meeks continued, everything fell apart. Mr. Gold closed his eyes, unwilling to visualize the scene his old friend was about to describe to him, and yet unable not to. Unable to not see the fierce rain pounding the highway, Dieter's bride driving home from her job at the university library, a car traveling in the opposite direction sliding across the center line and slamming into her Volkswagen head-on. Tragically, Meeks concluded in a near-whisper, Jennifer Rawls had been instantly killed.

So now you see, Mr. Gold explained to a clearly distraught Consuela that very same evening, why poor Mr. Dieter has chosen to flee his hometown and resettle, for the time being, right here.

And why he is so reticent about his personal circumstances. It is, no doubt, simply too painful to talk about, too painful to even think about.

When she began to sob, Mr. Gold wrapped an arm around the housekeeper's quivering shoulders and urged her to remain strong. She must pray for Mr. Dieter. They both must. So that one fine day, he concluded with sudden fervor, that estimable young man will pull himself up by the bootstraps and trod down the tenuous path to worldly happiness once again.

But Consuela was inconsolable, and that night she couldn't sleep. Her heart bled for the tragic writer, and her frustration soared. She racked her brains for some way to ease Dieter's pain, knowing that the best method to accomplish *that* little feat was through the healing power of love (or as the crude habitués of her neighborhood tavern liked to call it, a pity fuck), which was no longer a possibility now that Maggie Paterson had, without warning, burst upon the scene. Consuela wanted to take Mr. Gold's advice and be Christian about the entire matter but it was impossible not to imagine what would have happened if Maggie Paterson had minded her own business and stayed the hell away. Because I was here first, damnit, and if it wasn't for that redheaded hussy it would be me, not her, whose shoulder Dieter would be crying on right now!

As the sleepless hours ticked away into the blush of dawn, the housekeeper reviewed, over and over, her squalid romantic past. It was a train wreck: three ne'er-do-well husbands—one loser after another—and now Dieter, the man of her dreams, so near and yet so far away, in the clutches of a femme fatale. She locked a pillow between her legs and groaned, mourning her wretched fate, yet determined to remain vigilant just in case the torrid affair between the writer and the redhead eventually foundered on the jagged rocks of its own spontaneity, as affairs of that sort—rebounds— tended to do.

22

It might have been the change in the weather, the breeze that whistled off the harbor and tempered the blistering heat reminding him of the wind that sang in the cornfields once, under autumn's gibbous moon. Or it might have been something less tangible, a voice in a dream urging him to reconsider the merit of his decision to leave. Whatever the reason, one fall-like morning Dieter woke in his bed in room 24 positively homesick, missing, in particular, his dad.

As morning light poured through the room's open window he saw his father in the workshop sharpening his chisels, clamping a drawer front, mixing stains, a vision intimate and comforting until he noticed how tired and haggard the cabinet maker looked; then Dieter's soul ached, for he knew it was the son's absence that exacerbated the older man's sorrow, deepening his loss. He watched his father glance out the shop window at a wave of dark clouds curling over the hills of southern Indiana. In the garden, pumpkins lay scattered like beach balls next to a mound of winter squash, tomato vines clung to their trellis, a red wheelbarrow leaned against the door of its shed. And yet none of these familiar sights, Dieter suspected, infused in his father the sense of belonging he used to cherish, the understandable pride of a man who had come to Indiana with next to nothing to create a way of life that promised fulfillment but now seemed fleeting, insubstantial, nearly worthless. The land he once considered paradise huddled like a penitent beneath the brooding shadows of those clouds. Soon the cold rains would fall before freezing into snow, powdering the blue hills. Black ice, winter light, fear of aging. Mornings he would tramp out to the workshop as he always had but there would be no pleasure in it now, only duty; the son still absent, the daughter-in-law still dead.

Dieter squeezed a quarter into the payphone in front of the Gibson, asked the operator to reverse the charges, and waited for his father to answer the call.

I'm fine, Dad, just fine. Yes on both counts, he answered; he was eating well and exercising, too.

He described his morning walks down to the harbor and the afternoon swims off Christopher Key. In answer to the next question, he confirmed that he was still refinishing furniture two days a week in Frank Paterson's store, and when the line went silent, the son knew that the father was pondering once again why the boy was toiling for a stranger when he could be working right there, where he belonged.

What about money? Do you need any money?

No, Dad, I'm good. His agent had just wired him a thousand dollars to hold him over, he said. And there was plenty more where that came from. Not to worry, there was going to be more.

Another uncomfortable silence while Dieter waited for his father to voice, not for the first time, his doubts. Although he was justly proud of his son's success, it was difficult for the cabinet maker to understand the market forces that determined the worth of a book. A cabinet maker submitted a bid, and if the contract was awarded he calculated what the profit from the job would purchase (a new lawn mower, carpeting for the spare bedroom), or pay off (the equity line, the Home Depot bill). The market for a novel, on the other hand, was amorphous, unpredictable, impossible to pin down even when Dieter once again explained, with admirable patience, the equation. For every copy that sells, he said, I make a percentage. And the book is still selling, as you know, quite well. In addition, there had been an inquiry from one of the movie studios, some interest in a possible script.

But to the cabinet maker it all sounded, in the end, rather vague. He didn't trust easy money.

This agent of yours, he gets a percentage too, right?

Yes, Dad. It's how he makes a living.

Dieter wanted to tell him that he had woken up homesick today but admitting his own sadness would only fuel the older man's remorse, so he held his tongue. Because the father, like the son, suffered Jen daily, hourly, remembering every minute he'd spent with her in their short time. Escorting her down the trail behind the house that led back to the pond where Dieter used to fish when he was a boy, or dusting off the old family albums to point out the stern faces of his forebears, their Germanic austerity. Dieter clutched the phone, his mood darkening, his knuckles turning white. Six months had already passed but to the father, no less than the son, Jennifer's death remained untenable.

He hung up, slid another quarter into the metal slot, and dialed Laurie.

Her name?

Her name, Dieter. What is the woman's name?

Maggie. Maggie Paterson.

Laurie sighed. Fine. Now tell me how you met.

For the first time that day, thinking about Maggie, Dieter felt his homesickness loosen, slightly, its grip.

She saw me skinny dipping.

What?

Skinny dipping.

Where?

In her pond.

In her what?

In her pond! She has a pond!

I bet she does.

Careful now.

Well what the hell were you doing there? And why were you skinny dipping?

Because I was hot, he said flatly.

You were hot?

Um . . . duh. I'm in *Florida*?

Uh-huh.

Besides, I didn't know anyone was watching.

How romantic.

You'd have to ask her.

What he didn't tell Laurie was that his compulsion to possess—no, to *consume*—Maggie Paterson reminded him, worrisomely, of Erik Fuller, his fictional double in *Jaguar Moon*. Like Dieter during his time in Quintana Roo, Erik Fuller considered compromise an unworthy option, the path a sissy would choose. If you saw something you wanted, you took it. So when Fuller drank he drank, until the edges of the world blurred and the dark sand he trod home on turned gold in the light of the moon. When he swam he swam, until the muscles in his arms burned from exhaustion and his heart felt like it was going to explode. And when he made love he was so intense he often scared women away. In the kitchen of the hotel where he had labored during the day, Dieter tore chickens open with his bare hands and watched their blood pool on the stainless steel counter. Later, at the Yucatan Café, he picked up hippie strays—there were more than you could count—and took them back to his room on the outskirts of the village. Where in bed he turned into Erik Fuller, swordsman extraordinaire, whose bouts of lovemaking were nothing more than contests, conquests, a scorecard. In the morning the strays left early, pale as ghosts, with little to say. Nights of lust but nothing more, nothing deeper, nothing you could hang an actual emotion on. Until he met Jen.

He saw the look of surprise on Maggie's face the first time they made love and he wondered if it was fear. The second time he forced himself to slow down by imagining a ship negotiating a channel's narrow waters, reversing thrust, and afterwards Maggie's quiet contentment mirrored, briefly, his own. Despite his misgivings, tenderness, it seemed, was still possible. And yet minutes later, in the afterglow, he became agitated again. Why was he dragging poor Maggie into the maelstrom of his life? What right did he have to do that? In the old country, in his grandfather's country, a widower wouldn't have given another woman a second thought until a year had passed. And he wouldn't have run away, either. He would have trudged down to his workshop in the cold morning light to bend his body to humble labor, to repair a clock or mend a barrel or fashion, out of staves of black walnut, rifle stocks; to compose the opening passage of an aria or ink, across a sheet of parchment, the words *Chapter One*. What he wouldn't have done is fall into the arms of the first woman who hinted her possible interest. His hands trembled as they slid down Maggie's smooth flanks. To assuage his guilt, he tried to hide in her crevices, he tried to drown.

Come home, Dieter, his sister cried. That was an option, all right, but so was drowning, though he didn't tell Laurie that.

Bring her with you.

Drowning was an option and so was alcohol, or scag. The thought of getting high kindled a sudden thirst, a desire as elemental as breathing. He thought about the bureau in his room in Quintana Roo, before Jen: the bag of white powder, little silver spoon, pillboxes. There were tabs of mescaline Parrish brought back from Tampico, and bottles of bootleg gin. At dusk, Dieter would lie in a hammock on the beach or straddle a barstool at the Yucatan Café and watch the sun plunge into the water as various chemicals dissolved in his bloodstream, offering satiation. Getting high solved, among other issues, the question of why he wasn't as happy as he thought he should be down here among the expats. So he lit a hash pipe or swallowed a tab of acid or lifted a spoon to his nose and waited for the world to make sense again. And when the drug took hold he lay back in his hammock—painless now—to listen to a faint lisp of surf or later, on his stereo, a song by Fever Tree, that solemn flute.

He hung up the phone and crossed the street and strode into the Blue Moon with a new sense of purpose. Gene, who was wiping down the bar with a rag more soiled than whatever it was trying to absorb, shot Dieter a look, surprised to see an afternoon drinker, a happy hour type, so early in the day.

What's the haps, D?

Dieter scoped the room, pleased to find it empty. What he needed to do required a certain amount of privacy. He nodded at the coffeepot Gene was holding in his hand and waited for the bartender to pour each of them a cup. Then, before Gene even had a chance to set the coffeepot back down, he blurted out the question he had assumed, not so long ago, he would never ask again.

I don't know, man. Gene shook his head, apparently disappointed, as if the unexpected request had revealed a moral crack in Dieter's character. The bartender cradled his steaming cup in two hands and stared dully out the front door he had propped open that morning to let a little air in, a little light. And all of a sudden Dieter realized his mistake, his false assumption.

Look, Gene, I'm sorry I put you on the spot like this. I shouldn't have asked.

Nah, man, it's not *that*. Trust me, you're not the first one. What I meant is I really don't, like, know. 'Cause I don't fuck with that stuff anymore.

I hear you. Smart man.

Gene spilled some sugar into his mug and watched the spoon leave a tiny wake in the coffee. Yeah well, the thing is I used to have, you know . . .

Of course I know, Dieter responded. A habit, you had a habit, right? Hey, who didn't?

In Mexico, Dieter could have told him, there was a time when China White was his only passion, the one lover he remained faithful to. The writing had veered off track, sex with the strays had lost its allure, and he was stuck in a dead-end job in a dead-end town without a prospect in sight. He still clung to the idea that somewhere in the world there was a certain woman, a soul mate, who would reveal the possibility of tenderness, maybe even love, but for the time being, a needle sliding under his skin was the softest caress he could summon. After work he avoided the Yucatan Café and went straight home to his spoon, his lighter, and a notepad. And there, in the glow of a minor dose, which was all he could afford, he somehow took control of the book again, forcing himself to follow a strict regimen of fruits and grain and exercise while avoiding alcohol altogether, toiling in the hotel kitchen during the day and holing up in his room at night to finish his opus, monk-like, except for the occasional shot of smack. Then one evening Erik Fuller collapsed on a moonlit beach and blood streamed out of his mouth, staining the sand, and when Dieter finished writing that chapter he was shaking. He studied, in shame, the tracks on his arm, vowing to clean up his act before it was too late, before it was *his* blood, not Erik Fuller's, that blackened a Mexican beach.

Thanks for the coffee, Gene. He laid a five down on the bar and stood up to leave. Let's just forget I brought it up, okay?

Wait a minute, D. Not so quick, huh? Gene lifted his hands in surrender. Look, there's this guy I know. I could talk to him. No promises, okay? But I'll see what I can do.

Dieter nodded, knowing how this would work, how Gene the middleman would skim his own percentage off top. And why not? I appreciate this, Geno. I really do.

Forget about it. He picked up his bar rag. So what are you looking for, anyway? Smoke? Pills?

Dieter's lopsided grin seemed, to the bartender, almost feral, coming from such a gentle man. Anything you can get me, bro, anything at all.

Gene began to wipe down the counter again, alarmed by Dieter's parting words. *Anything you can get me, bro*; a flat, airy statement that sparked the bartender's suspicion and caused him, a few days later, to voice his concern. Not just the words, either, he would say, but the way the man had spoken them, as if the answer was so obvious the question didn't need to be asked. *Anything at all.*

Because in Gene's world, this was not the way it worked. He could recall half a dozen other patrons approaching him the same way Dieter had this morning, as furtive as men sneaking into a peep show, strangers stuck here in town for a few days wondering where they could score. Unlike Dieter, though, those men were always specific—hashish, seconal, meth—as precise in their choice of poison as customers who ordered Cutty Sark neat, or Jose Cuervo with salt and limes. Who in their right mind said *anything at all?* As if there was no difference between a harmless joint and a needle filled with scag. As if, when you came right down to it, the only issue was oblivion, and how fast you could get there, and who you took along.

23

No, it was a ten, Maggie repeated. Not a twenty, a ten.

It was a twenty.

I'm sorry, ma'am, but it was a ten.

Maggie refused to lower her gaze, even though staring down the customer—a fifty-something in a ratty housedress; who came out to a grocery store in the middle of the day in a housedress?—accomplished nothing. Maggie suspected the old shrew had fine tuned this particular scam on any number of cashiers, and wasn't about to be taken to task by this one.

She glanced up at Cain the Pain's glass-enclosed office on the second floor and saw the manager staring back down at her, already alerted. She held up the ten-dollar bill the woman had given her, and a few minutes later the Pain appeared at her side, inquiring, in a particularly cloying tone, if he could be of some service.

Maggie explained the situation then leaned insolently against her drawer, waiting for the Pain to do what he always did, to apologize to the old hag and hand her change for a twenty even though he knew it was highly unlikely that Maggie, as efficient a cashier as he had ever worked with, had miscalculated. The truth didn't matter; the customer, as everyone knew, was never wrong.

To add insult to injury, after handing the woman the incorrect change the Pain offered to escort her out to the parking lot. Where, with a nod and a wink, he opened the back door of her car, placed the paper sack on the floor, and wished her a wonderful day. Maggie fumed.

An hour later, when she was getting ready to go on break, the Pain appeared at her side again, sneaking up without warning this time. He bent over the register pretending to study her tape. But he was standing too close. She could smell his sour breath and feel his bony hip rubbing against hers. She was ready to snap, ready to grab the son of a bitch by the short hairs and inform him in no uncertain terms that if he pressed up against her like that one more time she was going to sue him and his beloved grocery chain for sexual harassment.

Dieter laughed when she told him the story but his face expressed concern, too, empathy. After a lively swim in the surf they were strolling down the dazzling white sands of the beach on Christopher Key.

Cain the Pain, huh. I think I saw him once. The skinny guy with black glasses, right? Oily hair, looks like it's plastered on?

That's the one.

Determined not to let the incident at work ruin the rest of her day, Maggie looped an arm through Dieter's and concentrated, instead, on her good fortune. On this exquisite fall afternoon— warm sun, pillows of cloud, a whisper of surf—here she was waltzing down a lovely stretch of sand with, of all people, her new lover. Her new lover! The word still felt clumsy on her tongue, in her mouth, whenever she said it. Boyfriend? No, that wasn't accurate either. She was momentarily flummoxed. What do you call two people who have just discovered an affinity in bed and now wonder if that passion will translate into something more? Already she had the feeling that it might. For one, the sex had been extraordinary—to Maggie's delight Dieter had proven himself a keen and attentive partner, orally inclined—but it was what happened in the aftermath of their initial lovemaking that truly surprised her. Still bristling with energy, Dieter had hopped out of bed and skipped across room 24 to retrieve two bottles of beer from a Coleman cooler he kept stocked with refreshments for moments, Maggie supposed, like this. And as she leaned back against the headboard, the man who had heretofore been known mainly for his reticence began to tell her the story of his life. After months of silence the floodgates burst open, and the memories came pouring out.

Maggie relaxed, listening to Dieter's unexpected narrative. A childhood in the hill country near Bloomington; the deep, abiding friendship with his sister Laurie; an apprenticeship in his father's workshop while he pursued, at night, his true calling, books. He read voraciously, he said, anything he could get his hands on: Hemingway, Faulkner, Pound. Like the early days in his father's woodshop, literature was a kind of apprenticeship, the wide-eyed novice dissecting certain sentences again and again to try and determine how the great writers locked those words together until they were as seamless as one of his father's dovetail joints. And even though he inwardly scoffed at the notion that someone like him might eventually write that well too, one day he decided it might be worth the effort, if only to confirm his doubts.

Not surprisingly, his initial attempts to emulate the masters were spectacular failures; an international spy novel hampered by the fact that he had never traveled beyond the Midwest; tortured love poems that sought to mimic, to no avail, the rhythms of Rilke; political rants. Repositioning the ladder, he returned to prose, but more modestly now, penning a series of concise, straightforward narratives—sketches, he called them—set in the hill country, featuring a young protagonist fashioned after Nick Adams in Hemingway's *In Our Time*. Determined to make his mark, however faint that mark might be, Dieter sent the stories out to the journals and received, for his efforts, so many rejection slips he began to wonder if his talent was a sham, a delusion.

And then one dreary December afternoon he trudged out to the mailbox through a foot of frozen snow to retrieve a letter that would effectively demolish this fatalistic view. Steeling himself for yet another rejection, Dieter sliced open the envelope only to discover, to his absolute astonishment, that one of his stories had been accepted for publication. He was a sophomore in college, still living at home, when the dam broke. Other stories were soon picked up—including one by the *New Yorker*—and a minor reputation, particularly around the IU campus, took root. Somehow, at twenty, the young writer had found his own voice, his own vision.

But as in any life, there were difficulties too: his mother's sudden death from a rare blood disorder the year Dieter turned thirteen; the ups and downs of his father's business; his sister Laurie's juvenile diabetes. To top it off, there was the increasingly strained relationship with his dad. They had always been close, but as Dieter's literary ambitions blossomed, the rapport between son and father collapsed. The cabinet maker wanted to know why Dieter wouldn't admit that earning a living scribbling words on paper was a pipe dream. It was a nice hobby, even a noble one, he declared, but the boy needed to be realistic about his goals.

Dieter seethed at his father's lack of understanding, his refusal to recognize his son's special gifts. In the following weeks there were long periods of brooding silence punctured by sudden verbal jabs, and finally the situation became intolerable, the skirmishes so frequent and heated, Dieter marched into the kitchen one morning to announce that he was moving to Quintana Roo. To write.

A wave larger than all the preceding ones broke on the shore, rinsing Maggie's ankles. She squealed with surprise, startled by the sudden foam. She hadn't been back to this particular beach in years. When she was a kid, Christopher Key remained undeveloped, pristine, a wonderland. She had learned to swim there, splashing in the surf with her mother and father, beguiled by the tide rolling in and out of the estuary, the sandpipers pecking at tiny crabs burrowing in the wet sand, the pelicans soaring over the breakers in long, graceful Vs. Later, out by the old saltworks, she had reclined in the back seats of a succession of Fords and Chevys with boys she wasn't all that fond of, necking until her lips turned blue. She had smoked pot there too, for the first time, with Jackie Banks. And hadn't been back since. Like many locals she avoided the island now that it had become an exclusive sanctum for the *nouveau riche*, even if some right-minded citizens had managed, bless their hearts, to save the northern beaches.

After another hearty splash in the Gulf—salty kisses, restless hands—Dieter drove her back into town so she could pick up Hunter at Lureen's and take him home. In a quiet voice she refused Dieter's offer to come with them. Hunter, she said, was still adjusting to Colt's absence and might not be ready yet to meet another man.

24

Lureen handed Maggie a Mason jar. Lipton, ice cubes, a wedge of lime.

Have some tea, sis. Take a load off.

They sat out by the pool watching Hunter and Toby play on the swings. It was a quiet, drowsy afternoon but Lureen was antsy today, bored with the usual banter. What she wanted, she told Maggie, was the dish on Dieter, her sister's new stud.

Maggie shook her head, refusing to gossip or gloat. I've got a better idea.

Oh yeah? What's that?

Read his book. It's pretty much all right there.

Lureen lifted a cautionary finger in the direction of Toby, who was hanging upside down from a high steel bar, imitating a marsupial. Speaking of which, Lureen said, her eyes still on Toby, I hear that book is kinda . . .

Maggie feigned innocence. Kinda what?

You know.

Do I?

Stop.

Oh, you mean racy?

Lureen turned back to her sister, grinning now. That's it, racy!

Well I guess you'll have to find that out for yourself. Or maybe you and Charley could read it to each other . . . in bed.

Lureen's laugh was a bark, an explosion. Like you and me used to read *Peyton Place*?

There you go.

Suddenly distracted, Lureen looked out at the boughs of a lemon tree heavy with fruit. Yeah, like *that's* gonna help she murmured, revealing, to her startled sister, an unexpected crack in the walls of her indomitable marriage. Maggie started to respond but Lureen, ever resilient, abruptly changed the subject, raising her glass for a toast. At any rate, she saluted, here's to the lovebirds.

Please.

Well that's what you two are, aren't you?

Friends, Lureen, we're just friends.

Uh-huh, sure you are. So where did you two . . . friends, go today?

To the beach.

Lureen set her jar down and rubbed the tips of her fingers together, ready to pounce.

Yeah?

Yeah.

And?

And what?

And what did you do!? Growing impatient, Lureen flapped her hands in the air like two broken wings. C'mon, sis, spill! Dish!

We did what most people do at the beach, Maggie calmly replied. We swam.

Deflated, but not ready to give up just yet, Lureen drummed her fingers on the armrest of her lounge chair. That's it?

Well no, not exactly. We ate some fruit, too, and took a long walk.

Maggie noticed that Lureen had polished off her tea and was chewing on an ice cube. Didn't someone say that chewing ice cubes was a sign of sexual frustration?

You ate some fruit, huh. Apples and such.

That's right.

How exciting, Lureen deadpanned.

Maggie glanced out at the back yard. On the swings, Hunter was hanging upside down now too, imitating his marsupial cousin.

Look, we're taking it slow, okay? A step at a time. We're both . . . well we're both, I suppose, a little frightened.

Lureen swallowed the masticated ice cube and frowned, mightily. Well phoo on you then, on both of you.

What Lureen wanted, Maggie concluded, was to remember what it felt like to fall head over heels in lust for a new man. In some corner of her mind Jesus had not yet taken total control of, she yearned to live vicariously through her badass older sister. As if all that sanctimony had begun, at last, to wear off. She misses it, Maggie thought. Born again or not, she misses it.

As she cruised through town, Maggie spotted Dieter crossing the street in front of the Gibson. She slowed to a crawl, rolling down her window. Hey there, stranger.

Hey yourself. Dieter leaned over, nodding through the jeep's open window at Maggie's passenger.

Dieter, this is my son Hunter. Hunter, this is Mr. Dieter. Mr. Dieter's a . . . he's an old friend. Dieter poked a hand through the window, grasping the boy's. Pleased to meet you, Hunter.

After a few minutes of careful small talk, Maggie waved goodbye and pulled away from the curb, failing to notice the man with stringy blond hair standing across the street in the shadow of an awning. The man had been watching them with great interest, noting how Dieter, while they talked, had reached out to rub Maggie's shoulder, an unmistakable gesture of intimacy.

When Maggie's jeep disappeared around the corner the man ambled down the sidewalk, pausing for a moment to peek into the window of the Blue Moon before stepping inside. He chose a stool near the door.

How you doin', Gene?

With a tremor of alarm—that voice was unmistakable—Gene glanced up from the newspaper he had been reading. Hey, Teddy. Long time no see.

Teddy Mink took a sip of the draft beer Gene set down in front of him, wiping the foam from his mouth with the back of a sleeve. His expression was, as usual, unreadable.

Since the tavern was otherwise empty, Gene felt compelled to remain at his end of the bar even though he didn't particularly want to. Teddy Mink made him nervous. He had a way of staring right through you, as if you weren't really there.

Tapping the side of his pint glass with a manicured fingernail, Teddy asked about the new guy in town, the one they called Dieter.

Come in here much?

Comes in all the time, Gene answered. He's stayin' right across the street, matter of fact, at the Gibson.

Is he now? Teddy took another sip of beer. Over the rim of the glass his cold blue eyes never wavered, never left the bartender's face.

Good customer? Big tipper? Good guy?

Yeah, he's a good guy, Teddy. Dieter's all right.

That's what I hear.

Teddy swiveled around on his stool to scan the empty room. He let the silence build. By inquiring about Dieter he had made it clear that even if Gene would have preferred small talk—how about those Bucs, Teddy?—this was not going to be an idle conversation.

So how's everything out—

Reason I ask? Teddy spun around to face the bar again. About this Dieter? Is I hear things, right?

Gene felt like a fish dangling on the barb of a hook. Things?

Yeah, you know, things.

The bartender hesitated, increasingly uneasy. Sorry, Teddy, guess I'm not following you.

Frightened by the drug lord's steely gaze, by his long silences and that sinister soul patch he had recently grown beneath his lip, the bartender looked away. He wanted to man up, but guys like Teddy Mink had always intimidated him. Not the authority figures but the ones who made those authority figures dance. Not the puppets like Howard Simmons or Captain Pursley down at the precinct, but the one who pulled their strings, the one who was sitting right here in the Blue Moon watching the bartender squirm.

Another beer, Teddy?

I don't think so, Gene. But hey, you know what I *do* need?

No idea, Teddy.

What I do need—and now Teddy leaned over the counter to emphasize the importance of what he was about to say—is a favor. The drug lord swallowed the rest of his beer. And all of a sudden he seemed as relaxed as a deflated balloon, as if the issue, whatever it was, had been resolved.

What kinda favor? Gene stuttered.

A simple one! I just want you to tell me what you know about this guy.

Gene's skin crawled. He thought about Dieter strolling into the bar the other day—*Anything you can get me, bro, anything at all*—and he knew that something was happening here he couldn't quite grasp. He imagined a net tightening around the stranger at the Gibson, a man who may or may not have been innocent. He imagined his own complicity in the affair.

But I don't know nothin', Teddy. Don't know a thing.

'Course you do, Gene. Teddy slapped his hand on the bar. You're a bartender!

Sure I am but . . .

Registering the look on Teddy's face—irritation but something more, something more than disdain, more than disappointment—the bartender choked on his own inadequacy. He feared he had gone too far. You didn't fuck around with guys like this. They could make you miserable. They could make you dead.

You know what *I* think, buddy? With a mean little twist of a grin Teddy took a folded fifty out of his wallet and placed it on top of the counter. What *I* think is that you and me better start over. Sound like a good idea?

Gene looked down at the money. If you believed the stories, behind the drug lord's casual demeanor—the sun-bleached hair, the muscle shirts and flip flops, the easy affability—lurked a stone cold killer. There were persistent rumors that refused to die, like the one about the two guys who crossed him on a deal in St. Petersburg and were found a few weeks later face down in Tampa Bay.

Teddy was waiting, a chessman who had just placed his opponent's king in check. Time was running out. It was the bartender's move.

Ashamed, conflicted, but mostly just scared, Gene reached out and picked up the fifty. His weakness seemed vast, his betrayal abhorrent.

Last time I saw him was Tuesday, last Tuesday.

Here?

Yeah, here.

And?

And he asked me, you know . . .

No, Gene—Teddy leaned back on his stool, at ease again—I don't know. Why don't you enlighten me.

25

Afterward, Nicky Meyers lay face down, naked, on her waterbed, skimming the National Enquirer while the dark paddles of a ceiling fan evaporated the beads of sweat goose-bumping her skin in the wake of the acrobatic, yet curiously unsatisfying, bout of lovemaking she had just engaged in. Ever the trooper, Nicky had given it her all, but as she rode the waves of Colt's mechanical pleasure she had sensed a certain distance, a shared emotional detachment, as if they were merely going through the motions even though they'd only been sleeping with each other for two weeks. Sometimes the initial shine wore off that quickly, not that this particularly bothered her. Soon Colt would flee—guys like him always did—and yet in light of the sheer number of attractive bodies out there available to a woman like her, there were, she reasoned, worse predicaments. She flipped through the tabloid, heaving a sigh, practically blissful; so many men, so little time.

Lying next to her, Colt shook his head in dismay, bewildered to be screwing someone who, in the afterglow, read the National Enquirer. He thought only little old ladies living alone in trailer parks on the wrong side of the tracks read that rag. With

Maggie there had at least been real books, paperback novels featuring intricate plots she liked to describe to him as they lay in the evening heat, sated. Those lost days that now seemed, in retrospect, a kind of Eden because nothing, really, had replaced them. Heaving his own sigh, he glanced across the bed as Nicky, captivated by a story about a UFO that had landed unannounced in Vatican City last week, followed the lines of type down the page with a polished fingernail, moving her silent lips.

To counter the vague but very real dissatisfaction that increasingly clouded his thoughts these days, Colt reminded himself that this would soon be over, all of it: playing house with the stripper, sleepwalking through his shifts down at the Black Kat Club, making nice with Teddy Mink. He counted the days till the next drug run, the *last* drug run, his growing anticipation like a chemical high. Seven days. Seven days until he headed south for the Keys without any intention of actually going there. Seven days until he cruised into Sarasota with a trunk full of powder to split with Eddie T. Seven days until he became, at last, a free man.

He slapped Nicky's bare ass and leapt off the bed. Gotta go, babe. Things to do.

What things?

Gotta see someone.

Gotta see who?

Jesus, it was worse than being married. Every time he left the apartment Nicky wanted to know where he was going and what he was planning to do. Even Maggie hadn't been this bad. Matter of fact, there toward the end Maggie didn't seem to give a damn *where* he went. Well, all that was about to change too. Show her the pictures, Eddie T. advised. The pretty as a postcard beach, the quaint little Mexican village, those wild parrots that nested like psychedelic pigeons in the bell tower of the Catholic church. Show her the pictures I sent you from the last time I went down. He leaned over and planted a kiss on Nicky's shoulder. Just a guy, babe. Be back soon.

Nicky tore her gaze away from a photo of the UFO hovering

over St. Peter's Square, her lips curling into the inauthentic sexual pout she bestowed on customers who stuffed five-dollar bills into her G-string.

You better, boy.

Colt slid into his Camaro and took off. Boy? Was that what he was to her, her boy? He had to laugh. For the first few nights of their ill advised affair, Nicky's bimbo behavior had seemed a small price to pay for the time they shared in the sack, but now even *that* had lost its appeal. For a bona fide airhead, the stripper was okay, sweet and muddled and harmless as a housefly. The problem was Colt didn't love her, he wasn't even sure he liked her that much. And in the long run, genuine affection was a must for a guy like him. What he had—has—with Maggie. What he feels for the kid.

He downshifted into second gear and swerved onto Fisher Point Road, heading out to his old high school. It was a flawless afternoon with shafts of light spearing down through clouds as buoyant as balloons but there was a weight in his heart that blinded him to such beauty. How many times had he cruised down this very road on his way to a game, a party, a date? How many times had he negotiated these tight curves with his arm around the shoulders of a curvy blonde? Even if the future held great promise—and it did, he kept assuring himself, it definitely did—the reason for his melancholy today was clear. Now that he was leaving his hometown for good, he was starting to realize that it was the one place he would miss, perhaps even mourn, in his long exile. But he didn't want to think about that now. He wanted to concentrate on the task at hand, because the plan was in place, time was running short, and he had to make sure there were no glitches.

Since it was Sunday afternoon, Gene's battered old Plymouth was the only other vehicle parked in the school lot. Colt climbed out of his car, noting how the high clouds above the somber central building darkened the windows of the classrooms and cast into shadow their lecterns, their blackboards, their tidy rows of desks. As usual, the sight of those antiseptic rooms provided a dose, in equal measure, of repugnance and pride. He was never much of a student, and his classes had been torture, but being the best athlete in his class had also lent him stature unmatched since. He remembered underclassmen whispering his name when he strode down the hallway, teachers patting him on the shoulder the day after a game.

He stepped around the corner of the gym and spotted Gene sitting alone in the bleachers that flanked the baseball diamond, sipping from a flask. Over the years, this ballpark had become their refuge, their comfort zone, a hallowed shrine with faded green bleachers where they could gaze out over the grassy field reminiscing about the good old days, two aging, undistinguished young men whose last shot at glory took place right here. On the pitcher's mound, in the batter's box, rounding the bases to the cheers of their hometown fans.

After his father's funeral, Colt found solace here by slamming back shot after shot of Southern Comfort until the cobwebs of denial were blown away by the horror of what had occurred, until he finally broke down and sobbed in front of his friend. And ever since, in times of trouble, and there were many, the two had returned. When Maggie announced her pregnancy, when Gene was fired for showing up drunk for work at the sawmill, the day before Colt's first drug run down to the Keys. It was here that Gene had admitted his darkest secrets, his addiction to smack and pornography as well as his complicity in a brutal sexual episode in the shower room at Raiford where he had been serving a six-month stint for passing bad checks. Here that Colt had listened to these depressing disclosures without comment or judgment before revealing a few of his own, because sinners needed confessionals, and this ball diamond was theirs.

As always, Gene raised his right hand to execute his half of their secret handshake but even that usually vigorous gesture seemed listless today. Clearly something was troubling the man. On the phone he had sounded nervous and strung out and now, in the unforgiving light of the sun, he looked awful, his eyes pouched and bruised from sleeplessness and worry. Had Tammy kicked his ass out again? Was he back on the junk?

As they passed the flask, Gene told him about his conversation with Teddy Mink, all those incessant questions.

About what?

About Dieter.

Who?

Dieter! The guy at the Gibson.

Oh yeah, right. The enigma. The mystery man.

Him.

Gene explained how Teddy had backed him into a corner, sliding a fifty across the bar.

I don't get it, Colt responded. Why all this interest in Dieter? Guy seems harmless, your basic flake.

Not to Teddy.

Colt took another swig from Gene's flask, wincing. He didn't know what was worse, the sting of Gene's cheap bourbon or the fact that he had called him out here to discuss something that seemed, what was the word, innocuous?

Not to Teddy?

Gene frowned. He genuinely loved this guy, always had, but sometimes Colt's inability to put two and two together drove the bartender nuts. Did he have to spell it out for him? Did he have to draw a fucking diagram?

Wait. Are you trying to tell me that Teddy thinks Dieter's a narc. A fucking narc?

Gene sighed—congratulations, Detective Poirot—while Colt squeezed his hands into fists and bit his lower lip, momentarily discombobulated. He didn't like where this conversation was heading, he didn't like it one damn bit. Seven days until he pulled off the deal of a lifetime and now this apparent complication, this possible wrench in the gears.

If Dieter *was* a narc, would Teddy back away? Would he cancel the next run? That would ruin everything. Eddie T. had already made the arrangements. The deal was in place. And what if it wasn't true? What if Dieter was just some chump kicking back in Crooked River because he didn't have anything better to do? What if this was just one more example of Teddy's legendary paranoia?

C'mon, Gene, are you sure about this? *That* goofy fucker? A narc?

I'm not sure about anything, Gene whined. I'm just telling you what happened. He polished off the last few drops in the flask before recounting how Dieter had strolled into the bar the other day, all smiles.

Is that how he said it? Where can I score?

That's how he said it all right.

And the next day, that's when Teddy came in.

You got it, chief.

Colt groaned, taut as a wire now. The local authorities wouldn't lay a hand on the kingpin—hell, half of them were on his payroll—but the feds were a different kettle of fish. Every few years the suits paid lip service to their masters by dropping a dime on players like Teddy Mink. They understood better than anyone that nothing was going to staunch the flow of coke—the market was simply too large, and too lucrative—but an occasional high profile bust made for good press, and helped secure their pensions. Was Dieter their front man? In a way he fit the bill: cipher, enigma, mystery man. In Colt's experience that was exactly what narcs were like, ingratiating, unknowable, and stealthy as sharks. But still . . . Dieter?

What I wanna know, Geno, is what *you* think, not Teddy, you.

About what?

About Dieter!

The bartender gazed out over the diamond at the centerfield fence. His eyes were bleary, his words a little slurred; he'd been drinking since noon.

I don't know *what* to think. At first I figured it was bullshit, you know? But then I started to look at it from Teddy's point of view. Guy shows up out of nowhere, drinks with the deckhands, gets cozy with the bartenders, starts askin' questions. Wants to know where he can score. You gotta look at the angles. I mean why would someone like that stay here for so long, in fucking Crook? He wants to get high, why wouldn't he go down to Miami, down to Tampa Bay?

He likes small towns, Colt replied, but Gene wasn't buying it.

He likes the slow pace, the quiet beaches.

Gene wasn't buying that either. He had learned a long time ago to trust his basest instincts. That was how you survived places like Raiford. If it felt wrong, it probably was.

I'm tellin' you, Colt, I'm gettin' a little nervous here, and you should be too. I don't need this shit on my conscience right now.

What shit?

Look, if he's a narc he's already too close. To me, to you, to all of us. And if he isn't . . . well if he isn't, what if Teddy whacks him anyway?

Jesus, Gene, what are you talkin' about, man?

Whose fault would *that* be? Mine, that's who.

Colt grabbed the flask but it was already empty. His mind was racing, looking for a foothold. Let's slow down here, huh. Let's stop and think about this.

Coincidence, Gene said, shaking his head. He was staring out past the centerfield fence at a chestnut mare grazing a distant pasture. I don't believe in it, you know?

Who does?

The way he holes up in that hotel room.

He's a loner. So what?

The way he won't tell nobody nothin'.

He's got secrets. Who doesn't?

And now this thing with Maggie.

As a swift cloud passed across the sun and a sudden breeze riffled the grass of the outfield, Colt squinted at the bartender. He figured he must have misheard him.

This thing with Maggie?

Gene shrugged, assuming Colt already knew; everyone else seemed to. Then he remembered that Colt had been out of town for awhile, on a drug run. Instinctively he raised his hands, as if to protect himself, because Colt's voice had already gone flat, the way it did right before he hit someone, or slashed a broken bottle across their face.

The fuck you talking about, man? What thing?

26

On Tuesday morning Dieter climbed into his pickup to drive out to Christopher Key. He was wearing cargo shorts, hiking boots, an IU T-shirt. In his backpack was a bottle of water, two banana muffins from the Delta Café, and the hiking guide he'd picked up the day before at the library.

So you're a hiker too, huh?

Well . . . sort of.

Man in the wilderness battles the fierce elements, fighting for his life.

That's me.

Our intrepid adventurer.

Dieter had laughed, following Jackie Banks down the stacks, amused by the librarian's inability not to flirt with him even though he knew that Dieter was not only straight as an arrow, he was also sleeping with Jackie's best friend. They paused in front of the 790s. Let's see now, hiking. Jackie's eyes raked the spines. Somewhere close, right?

Sure. Why not?

The librarian held Dieter's gaze for a moment, gauging

whether the writer's flip reply concealed an unsavory, and heretofore undiscovered, facet of his character. The other night when Jackie and Maggie had invited him out for drinks at the Holiday Inn, Dieter had noticed how protective Jackie could be around Maggie, presumably determined not to let any further harm—he refused to even mention Colt Taylor by name—befall her.

Yeah, the librarian finally acceded, why not? Then he grinned, loosening up a bit. Maggie was a big girl now and she could take care of herself. Besides, any way you cut it, William Dieter was a vast improvement on Colt.

So what about that trail out on Christopher Key? Isn't that where you like to swim?

Dieter nodded, amused. Did *everyone* in town know his personal habits? Or was this just idle gossip, what Maggie and Jackie dished out over their fruity tropical drinks when Dieter wasn't around.

I didn't know there *was* a trail on Christopher Key.

Sure there is, and it's a good one, too. Goes out to the marsh. Lots of birds for one thing. If you like birds.

A prick of pain as Dieter recalled Jen's enthusiasm. He saw her consult her trail guide, listen to the calls, repeat the lovely names: Swainson's warbler, red-tailed hawk.

Let's see now. Jackie retrieved a slender volume from the stacks and scanned the index. Here it is. Have a look.

Dieter read the description of the trail: 2.3 miles of moderate terrain with views over the marsh, including a short boardwalk across the shallows.

Sounds great. He clapped the big man on the back. Thanks, Jackie, I owe you one.

Oh yeah? The librarian dangled a wrist in playful mockery. One what?

At the bar in the Holiday Inn, Jackie had broken the ice by asking Dieter his opinion of certain books by authors they happened to share a passion for. Paul Bowles, Frederick

Exley, Philip Roth. As the day's last light waned in the picture-glass windows and the sunbathers around the pool retired to their rooms, the three of them settled in, discussing literature, something Dieter hadn't had the opportunity to do since the day he arrived in town. Eventually the conversation circled back to Dieter's own book, which caused some discomfort, for Dieter was one of those writers who didn't know how to react when fans praised his work. This time, however, he needn't have worried, because Jackie refused to fawn, asking precise, pointed questions instead, about the village in Quintana Roo, whether Parrish was based on an actual person (no, Dieter said, he was a composite), and if Erik Fuller's disastrous acid trip was fashioned after one of his own (yes). For all his flirtatious banter, the man was a serious and knowledgeable reader, which made his appreciation of *Jaguar Moon* genuinely flattering.

Ice broken, the rest of the evening passed amicably by in an alcoholic haze, the drinks flowing like water while Maggie leaned back in her chair content to listen to the two men talk, immensely pleased that her new beau had been charmed, just as she had hoped he would be, by her flamboyant friend. Colt the homophobe had always scoffed whenever Maggie suggested inviting Jackie out for dinner. What would we talk about for Christ's sake, he's a fucking twink! Conversely, Dieter had welcomed him with open arms, literally. As they were leaving the bar he had given a startled Jackie an affectionate hug before declining his offer of a ride back to the Gibson. He was pleasantly soused, he said, and it had been a wonderful evening, but he wanted to walk back to the hotel by himself, to stroll along the harbor, to enjoy the evening air.

Now as he drove across the causeway to Christopher Key, Dieter tracked a schooner chugging out past the channel markers into the open sea for its day of fishing. The sky was clear this morning and the first rays of light showered the harbor, sparkling on the hulls of the boats. He rolled down his window, smelling the salt in the air and remembering how Maggie tried to mask her disappointment when he declined Jackie's offer of a ride back to the Gibson the other night. He'd walked her out to Jackie's car and given her a long, affectionate kiss. I'll see you in the morning, okay? And I'll be thinking about you too.

You will?

All night long.

You promise?

He hung a left at the end of the causeway, the jarring display of indiscriminate wealth that desecrated the southern half of Christopher Key immediately plunging him into a cynical mood. While the northern end of the island remained more or less in its natural state, the southern half represented, to a man like Dieter, everything that was wrong with indiscriminate growth. Daunting white McMansions towering over thin strips of sand riprapped and sandbagged to prevent the erosion the developer's bulldozers had set into motion in the first place; stumps of native palms mercilessly toppled to make way for a three-car garage; privacy fences blocking views of the sea. At least the marsh had been protected. He consulted his trail guide. According to the map, the trailhead was on the left, just past the severe curve in the road he was now negotiating. Slowing down, he peered out the dusty windshield but couldn't spot it. Then he noticed a pullout of sorts, a rutted lane overhung with spindly branches. Maybe the trailhead sign was missing. Maybe this was it.

He eased the truck into the lane, parting the branches with the hood. A few feet on, the overhanging boughs began to thin out and then the trees ended, exposing a weedy clearing wide enough for him to turn back around and park, facing forward, on the shoulder of the road.

After maneuvering the truck into position, he grabbed his backpack and set out toward the marsh. The sun had yet to top the trees that defined the edge of the hammock he was about to cross, and even out here, under the wide blue sky, the air remained cool. He established a steady, methodical pace, one step at a time, on the trail that divided the grassland. Then he entered the next canopy and emerged a few minutes later to his first view of the wetland. As if in greeting, a cloud of white egrets rose from the reflective shallows, wheeling across the sky. Remembering how Jennifer used to react to such a sight, glassing the horizon with a look of joyful expectation on her face, he fished through his backpack for the binoculars, only to discover that he had left them in the truck.

27

When D.B. Harmon was on a roll like this, all you could do was wait him out, wait until he grew tired of his own tedious voice, wait until he returned, roundabout, back to the reason he'd phoned in the first place.

Way I see it, Ted, that boy's okay. Maybe not as ambitious as you and me but hey, that's a good thing, right? I mean how many are?

Teddy Mink winced, squeezing the phone in irritation. He didn't like it when anyone, even a client as wealthy as Dub Harmon, called him Ted. The name was Teddy.

No sirree, not like you and me, pal. Guys like us pulled ourselves up by the bootstraps, right? Same way our parents did. Down there in old Miami B.

Teddy skipped a reply even though he didn't exactly disagree. Not that a little silence, he supposed, would deter a guy like Harmon. Now that he'd mentioned his parents and South Beach in the same exorbitant breath, the realtor wouldn't be satisfied until he connected all the dots, and sure enough, that's exactly what he proceeded to do, going all the way back to that bumfuck hometown of his up there in Wisconsin (or was it Illinois?), his lack of college because his parents couldn't afford to send him to one, and finally that first fateful trip down to old Miami B, where money seemed to hang off the boughs of all those sparkling citrus trees.

That first magical million, Dub crowed, the year we met, remember? Height of the boom?

Like Dub, Teddy had made his first fortune in shady south Florida land grabs before moving on to even shadier, and more lucrative, ventures. Holding the phone a few inches away from his ear he peered out the window of his office at a pretty young thing strolling down the beach in a red bikini, impatiently waiting for Harmon to run out of breath or become bored with his own self inflation.

Anyhoo, like I said, Ted, that boy's okay, dependable. Did I tell you what he told me when he came down?

Teddy, who had nearly dozed off during Dub's mind-numbing personal saga, perked back up.

The boy?

Right, the boy.

Okay then, they were back on familiar ground now, back on code, the way the drug lord preferred it. Because you couldn't be too careful these days; after Watergate, you never knew when someone might run a tap on your lines.

No, Dub, I don't believe you did.

Well what he said was that he might be interested in buying a place down here.

Silently, Teddy forgave the realtor for wasting the last ten minutes of his life. No kiddin'. He say where?

Big Pine. Said he likes the area around that old boatyard, the one I'm thinking about dividing into lots.

Lots?

You remember; two lots steada one?

Oh yeah, right, *two* lots.

Teddy smiled, satisfied now. The deal was set and it was better than he had expected; double the weight, double the cash. Listen, Dub, I appreciate you calling, hear?

No problem, Ted.

The drug lord hung up, cringing again. Ted? The name's Teddy you fuckin' dork. Or better yet, Mr. Mink. On the other hand, the big man was *doubling up* this time. How sweet was that?

Teddy unlocked his desk drawer, withdrew an address book, and confirmed the number for Bogota. After haggling for a few minutes with the international operator, he waited for the prerecorded message to come on, which allowed him time to tap in his figures. A contented sigh as he hung up the phone. It was like placing an order for groceries down at the corner market, almost *too* damn easy.

Gazing out the office window (where had that blonde in the red bikini run off to, anyway?) Teddy reflected on just how bizarre this business of his was. In a matter of hours, down there in some dense Columbian jungle, men in fatigues would begin to position the product. In the dark, a panel truck would wind along a dusty track to the airstrip, where the pilot would be waiting. Then the powder would move north, south, then north again, eventually spreading out to a network of cities in little plastic baggies stepped on again and again until some poor schmuck in a coldwater flat paid through the nose to put up *his* nose what five steps back had been pure coca. What a lark this would be if it weren't illegal, if he didn't have to worry that one day he'd wake up with half a dozen pistols in his face.

He dialed Pam Morgan. Hey there, Pamela, how ya doin'?

Well if it isn't Mister Teddy fuckin' Mink.

The drug lord grinned. Sounded like Pam the souse was hitting the bottle a little early today, which for some perverse reason pleased him. What, after all, did the poor woman have to stay sober for? A deckhand from Everglades City who had been drinking just as much as she had to stumble down her driveway tonight hoping to get a little on the side? If she'd chugged enough hooch, she was likely to oblige. All that coke might have ruined Pam's sinuses and emptied her bank account, but it hadn't dampened her sexuality one damn bit. On the downside of forty she still enjoyed, make that craved, an occasional roll in the hay. Trouble was she pined for Teddy, always had, no matter how many times he rejected her.

He recalled the last time he'd gone down; the dead water in the salt flats, mosquitoes the size of palmetto bugs, and that heat! Hell, if I was her I'd slug back a few too. The truck runnin' okay?

The truck?

Yes, Pam, he repeated patiently, the truck. Christ, had she already forgotten that *truck* was the trigger, the key that unlocked the code? Otherwise you were still outside the circle, merely chatting.

Oh right, right, the *truck*.

Down in Miami, back in the glory days, Pam's idea of the good life was a few bumps in a bathroom stall at the Kennel Club followed by dinner with Teddy at Joe's Stone Crab: hush puppies, a bottle or two of Mums, and a veritable mountain of those delectable crustaceans—the finest on the planet— swimming in their buttery broth. So what if her appetite was shot? The champagne was superb, the conversation appropriately flamboyant, wild and crazy sex later that evening, if she didn't pass out first, a distinct possibility.

Reason I ask? Last time I drove it it sounded kind of ragged, like it might need a tune-up or something.

Sure, Teddy, I'll take it in.

How about I give Jake a call, down the garage, make the appointment for you.

Works for me.

Next Tuesday?

Say what?

Teddy glanced at his wristwatch. Ten o'clock in the morning and she was already plastered, too slow on the uptake to catch these basic prompts. Still, he loved this part, even the missed signals. It reminded him of a James Bond movie, Blofeld petting the big tomcat, talking trash to his thugs.

Tuesday the eleventh, okay? It was like trying to have a discussion with a child distracted by a cartoon on TV. Got it?

Got it. The eleventh.

Maybe you should write it down.

I'm writing!

Great. Now listen, honey, you be good.

Teddy?

He hung up before she had a chance to ask him when he was going to come down again—yeah, like *that* was gonna happen any time soon—before she started whining. Sometimes, out of nowhere, she burst into tears. Poor woman just couldn't handle her liquor anymore.

In the laundry room he scooped a generous helping of dry chow into Pepsi's bowl and carried it out to the dog run. Hearing his footsteps, the Rottweiler stretched awake, blinking at her master with big red watery eyes.

He knelt down and rubbed the dog's ears. You ready for your walk, girl, ready to go scare up some squirrels? Now that he had taken care of business, Teddy felt a rising optimism brighten his day. He attached a leash to Pepsi's collar, unlocked the gate, and started down the path that bordered the coastal road and led to the trail that looped back to the beach, their usual morning romp.

Holding on for dear life to Pepsi's leash, Teddy thought about last night, remembering why in addition to the upturn in business there was another reason for his upbeat mood today. After going over some figures with Howard Simmons in his office overlooking the bay, he had stopped at The Tides for a nightcap. Where, while sitting alone at the bar, he'd overheard a table of deckhands talking about Dieter.

The one wearing a Red Sox baseball cap demanded center stage.

I *told* you he was some kinda writer.

Nah, man, I was the one told *you* that.

Whatever, dude.

Not letting on that he was eavesdropping, Teddy sipped his drink, intrigued. A writer?

What kinda writer, a third deckhand asked.

Stories. Writes stories. Writes books.

No shit. Who knew?

Well for one, the guy in the ball cap cried, I did!

Teddy yanked on the leash, trying to stifle the dog's headlong momentum. Up ahead, on the opposite side of the road, a blue pickup was parked underneath the overhanging foliage but Teddy was too lost in his thoughts to register this. A writer? Could it be that simple? Could Dieter have come down to Crooked River to gather material for his next book? That's what the deckhand in the ball cap claimed, and as far as Teddy knew he may have been right.

When he got back home from The Tides he called a reporter he used to hang out with in South Beach. Had he ever heard of a writer named William Dieter?

Sure, the reporter replied, he wrote *Jaguar Moon*.

What's *Jaguar Moon*?

A novel.

Oh yeah? You've read it?

I have.

And?

Killer stuff, man. The real deal.

So Dieter was a writer after all. Which might just explain everything. Why he'd come down to Crooked River in the first place, and why he'd hooked up with Maggie Paterson. For one thing, Maggie was a reader, so naturally she'd be attracted by a writer with the credentials Dieter apparently possessed. He was good looking, too, maybe not as dashing as Colt Taylor but so what? Besides the physical attraction there was intellectual stimulation to consider also, something Maggie's life had surely lacked since the day she shacked up with Colt. *His* idea of a good read was the back of a box of Wheaties.

And yet . . . keeping a firm hold on the leash to prevent Pepsi from bolting, Teddy considered the other side of the coin. Being a writer might explain what Dieter was doing there. It might even explain his affair with Maggie Paterson. But what about his asking Gene where he could score? Obviously writers were just as susceptible to a drug habit as anyone else, maybe more so, but the incident still bothered him, just as it had apparently bothered Gene. Mexico, the bartender had groaned. Maybe what, he got busted down there? Those *federales*, man. Way I hear it those fuckers can put the screws in good.

What are you saying? Teddy had asked.

I'm not saying anything.

You're saying he cut a deal.

I'm not saying anything!

Hey!

Without warning, Pepsi yanked on the leash with all her strength, nearly ripping it out of Teddy's hand. She was straining to cross the road, having likely caught the scent of an animal in the woods over there, a raccoon or a possum or one of the feral cats that hung out in the brush.

Stop! In response to Pepsi's sudden enthusiasm, Teddy yanked just as hard on the other end of the leash, choking the Rottweiler into submission. At the same time, the blue pickup camouflaged by all those overhanging branches finally caught his attention. Now what the fuck, he thought, is this? The truck was parked in a shadowy pullout no one, in Teddy's memory, had ever used.

He eyed the pickup with mounting suspicion. It could, he supposed, belong to a hiker on his way to the marsh, or maybe some kids heading back to the boardwalk to get high. But why would anyone park here when the trailhead, and its gravel lot, was no more than a hundred yards farther down the road?

After tying Pepsi's leash to the spindly trunk of a slash pine, he peered through the windshield. There was nothing lying on the seat, no gun rack in the back window, nothing to identify who the owner of the vehicle might be. He tried the passenger door and discovered, to his surprise, that it was unlocked. Glancing around the woods to make sure the hiker, or whoever it was, wasn't lurking, he unlatched the glove compartment and peeked inside. And when he saw what the glove compartment contained—a pocket notebook, a ball point pen, and a pair of binoculars—his pulse began to race and his mouth went dry.

He scanned the notebook, frowning at the cramped handwriting, the flurry of indecipherable words. Then he rifled through the glove compartment again, looking for the truck's registration, which, to his dismay, wasn't there. Didn't everyone leave their registration in the glove compartment? Something was wrong, something was definitely wrong. He tried, once more, to imagine why anyone would park here and came up blank. It made no sense, unless that is, unless . . . To confirm his darkest suspicion he circled back around to the driver's side of the truck to determine what someone with binoculars would see from there, and sure enough, what he would see, through an opening in the overhanging boughs, was Teddy's mansion.

A few minutes later he stood at the window of his second-story bedroom gazing down at the pickup. He liked to consider himself relatively fearless but this was cold sweat time. Someone was watching him. Someone who wanted to do him harm. And sooner or later that someone would step out of those woods, climb back into that pickup, and reveal who he was.

28

Now that Teddy Mink had grown one of those preposterous soul patches underneath his lower lip, Colt finally figured out who he was trying to look like: not a California surfer but Gregg Allman, the southern blues singer with the golden pipes. Not that Teddy, at his age, could pull it off; there were too many miles on that particular tread. Still, leave it to the only guy Colt knew who was vainer than him to try.

He swiveled around in his poolside chair to study, in the sliding-glass doors, his own pleasing reflection. Unlike Teddy Mink, Colt thought, I can be anyone at all. Don a denim vest and a pair of alligator boots and voila, southern outlaw. Top my dome with that new white Stetson and there you have it, western rogue. Hell, if I bought a pair of eurotrash sunshades and tooled around town on a Vespa, I could even pass for one of those gigolos in *La Dolce Vita.*

The back door swung open and Teddy stepped out onto the deck. He handed Colt his drink and sat down across from him.

So where was he?

Where was who?

Colt took a generous swallow of the drug lord's excellent scotch. Dieter. If he was surveilling, why wasn't he in the truck?

How the fuck should I know? Maybe he was taking a piss. Maybe he walked back to the marsh to check the birds out. Who the fuck cares?

There you are then. The birds.

What?

Colt knew he was grasping at straws, but what other choice did he have? The birds, he said. Maybe he was checking out the birds. There's a bunch of 'em back there.

I see. Teddy gazed out at the beach, which was deserted today. Herons and all, he said. Anhingas.

I just meant . . . Teddy's blistering look stopped the mule in his tracks. He lowered his eyes, unable to meet the drug lord's cold, uncompromising glare.

You meant?

That we should look at all the angles, Colt muttered.

The angles.

Yeah.

Fine. Teddy drummed his restless fingertips on the tabletop. So what are we saying here? What's the angle? What am I supposed to believe? That out of everybody in town Dieter's the one who just happens to park his pickup across the road? Because he's some kind of ornifuckinthologist?

We aren't sayin' anything.

First time I ever saw a vehicle there, pal. First time.

The bottom line was simple. Teddy wanted Dieter dead and he wanted Colt to make it happen.

Binoculars.

Right there in the glove compartment.

And a notebook.

Teddy nodded.

You took a look.

I took a look! Lot of fuckin' scribblin', couldn't read a fuckin' word.

To lighten the mood, Colt took a weak stab at humor. A writer who can't write, musta flunked penmanship.

Yeah well, he's gonna flunk somethin' else, too. Real soon.

Somethin' else?

Breathin'.

Colt took another hefty gulp of Teddy's scotch, trying to drown his trepidation. He might be tough as nails when it came to a Saturday night brawl down at the Black Kat Club, but he was no killer. No way.

I don't know, Boss. This is bad, man, this is really bad.

Tell me about it.

By arranging to have Colt handle the hit, Teddy, as usual, would shield himself from the law. Look, I'm not asking you to do it yourself, okay? I'm just asking you to find someone who will.

A hit man?

Whatever.

Like I know someone like that? Colt cried. C'mon, Boss, I'm a *bouncer*!

With a cryptic smile Teddy looked out at the sea again; gray breakers under a gray sky pierced, now and then, by shafts of light. But you do, he said quietly. That's the thing, you do.

Colt shook his head. How he hated this place. Every time he was summoned here there was more awful news. Do I?

Sure you do. Think Mexican.

Mexican?

Think beer bottle.

Colt's mind reeled. Who the fuck was Teddy talking about now, Jimmy Santiago? There was no way. Jimmy couldn't kill a man any more than he could.

Think gold tooth.

Colt set his drink down, staring in dismay at the kingpin. He couldn't believe what Teddy was suggesting. You gotta be kidding?

Do I look like I'm kidding?

No, but—

Two thousand.

What?

Two grand. Split it any way you want.

Colt sighed, on the verge of surrender. Once again Teddy had backed him into a corner he wasn't going to be able squeeze out of. What else could he do but obey the order, no matter how distasteful that order might be? He couldn't kill Dieter himself and he didn't know anyone else who could either, except perhaps Raul.

As he drove back into town the logistics of the job consumed him. And then, all at once, he had a revelation. The rip off wasn't going to be that difficult but convincing Maggie to follow him down to Mexico was another matter. Why hadn't he grasped back at Teddy's how convenient it would be to have Dieter out of the way? With her lover dead and gone, surely Maggie would be open to his offer. What could be better, after such a tragic event, than to get the hell away?

Psyched now, he considered the arrangements. First he'd call a meeting with Jimmy and Raul, ostensibly to clear the air. With as much humility as he could muster, he would admit that he never should have cut Jimmy in the first place, and that he deserved the punishment he'd received. An eye for an eye and a tooth for a tooth, he'd say; which meant they were all square now, right? Then, to show good faith, he'd offer Raul the contract. A grand for the hit? No, let's make it fifteen, he was feeling generous today. Generous, magnanimous, full of love for those enemies who would get rid of the final obstacle on the path that would lead, ultimately, to his freedom.

A few days ago, when Gene let slip the news about Maggie and Dieter, Colt had been furious. First she kicks him out of the house and then she betrays him with someone she barely knows. He had lain in bed that night unable to sleep, his mind a black fury. But what could he do? If he confronted Maggie about the affair she'd laugh in his face. Why don't we talk, she'd say, about Nicky Meyers? If he mentioned Mexico she would assure him that she wasn't going anywhere, with him or anyone else. So he'd tossed and turned for the rest of the night waiting for dawn, tormented, sleepless, crazed. The deal was due to go down any day but without Maggie and the boy, what was the point?

Then Teddy had called, offering his mule—who was too stressed out to recognize it as such—a solution. To ease Maggie's grief, Colt would offer her a shoulder to cry on, and when her sobs subsided he would make his pitch. In a soothing voice he would tell her about Mexico, the parrots in the palm trees, the murmur of the surf at daybreak, the chapel where she could light a candle for Dieter's lost soul. This is your chance, he would whisper, to heal those wounds. Why stay here, surrounded by all these terrible memories?

A trial period, that's what he would call it. Quiet time in a quiet place where she could relax, regroup, and eventually make the most important decision of her life: whether to return to a dead-end job in a dead-end town or to remain right there, in paradise, with the man she was meant for all along.

29

Even when they were kids Lureen didn't like to bait her own hook, wrinkling her nose in repugnance whenever the earthworm squirmed away from the barb, attempting again and again to spear that little sucker until she finally gave up and begged Maggie, at ten already a tomboy, to do it for her. And now here they were again, twenty years later, reenacting the very same scene.

Jesus, Lureen, it's only a worm.

Please don't use His name in vain like that, Mag.

Oh yeah. Sorry.

No shrinking violet, Maggie deftly hooked the worm through twice so it wouldn't wiggle away as soon as the bobber hit the water, recalling how their father used to take her and Lureen out to the Wakulla River to fish. The sun sparkling off the feathery stems of a tangle of reeds as Frank taught them to release their lines at the top, to let the weight of the leader spin out from their shoulders until it arced into the water, pulled taut by the current thirty feet downstream. The sudden tug of a fish followed, seconds later, by a yelp of joy. On a portable grill propped over the coals of a campfire, the skins of the filets charred black, their juices sizzling on the embers.

Today, if they were lucky enough to catch a few perch, Maggie would roll the filets in corn meal the way Frank had taught her and pan fry them on the stove. In deference to little sister, she would skip the Chardonnay.

Still thinking about those halcyon days on the river, Maggie heard the rattle of an engine and looked up in time to see Dieter's pickup pull into the drive. She hadn't been expecting him. Her heart began to hum.

Well now, Lureen murmured salaciously, look what the cat dragged in.

Easy there, sis.

Soon Dieter was sitting between them casting his own line into the shallows while Lureen chattered away about anything and everything that popped into her head. A good-looking man could still unnerve her, particularly today.

Earlier, on the phone, she had announced that there was a matter of "some delicacy" she wanted to get off her chest, and she didn't know who else to turn to.

Bring your rod and reel, Maggie replied. We'll catch us some perch.

On the dock it didn't take long for Lureen to explain that the delicate matter she so urgently needed to address was her growing dismay over the recent lack of passion in her marriage. With all of Maggie's experience, she was hoping for some helpful advice.

Experience carried a faint odor but Maggie decided not to take offense. Talk to me, she said.

According to Lureen, and who better to pass judgment, Charley was a wonderful father, a wonderful provider, a wonderful man. Up until a few months ago he had also been rather wonderful in bed. Not particularly imaginative, she admitted, but always there for her, ready to give it another go. And then something happened, and all of that changed.

What?

What what?

What happened?

I don't know!

Then how do you know?

Know what?

That something happened!

Because, Lureen whimpered, he's stopped, you know . . .

Sleeping with you? Frowning, Lureen flicked her line into the pond. That phrase, she said. I've never understood it. I mean it's not exactly *sleeping* we're talking about here, right? *Sleeping* ain't the issue.

Displeased with her sister's sudden snippy attitude, Maggie said fine. Fucking you? He's stopped fucking you?

Maggie!

What?

Even though Lureen was irritated, if not particularly surprised, by Maggie's vulgarity, her displeasure paled in comparison to the bewilderment Charley's recent indifference had provoked. His passivity was enough to make a wife, even a born-again one, suspicious. And yet she just couldn't feature good time Charley playing around. Who would want the big oaf?

Maggie trod, more softly this time, across the broken glass. So have you tried . . .

What?

You know.

To spice things up? Lureen shook her head. Trust me, honey, I've tried all right. Every trick in the book.

Although she didn't really want to, Maggie pictured lacy negligees, whipped cream, fellatio. It was not a pretty sight. Fortunately, at the same time these disturbing images streamed through her mind, Dieter's pickup skidded into the drive.

And now here he was, watching the bobber out of the corner of his eye and smiling dutifully while a nearly-manic Lureen described a trip she and Charley had taken to Guatemala last year, a busload of born agains bringing to the heathens of the highlands the word of the Lord. Maggie watched Dieter carefully, knowing his disdain for evangelical fervor. He had seen this movie before, in Quintana Roo. What those poor people need, he would tell you, wasn't the Book of Job, but dentists, water treatment plants, agricultural engineers. And yet to Maggie's great relief—the last thing she needed right now was an argument about religion—Dieter, with the patience of Job, held his tongue.

When Lureen finally ran out of breath they fished for awhile in silence, listening to the whirr of dragonflies hovering inches above the pond. Eventually, having snagged half a dozen perch between them, they went back to the kitchen where Maggie seasoned the filets while Lureen whisked the salad dressing and Dieter mixed a second pitcher of iced tea.

Staring out the window at the far wall of trees casting its shadow across the pond, Maggie felt a rush of affection for all living things. For Dieter and her sister, for Hunter and his towheaded schoolmates, for the mayflies dimpling the water and the deer hiding shyly in the cedars and the souls of the perch they were about to consume. There were times lately when life seemed, against all odds, downright enchanted.

Hey, Mom!

Maggie spun around as Hunter pranced through the door, waving at his mother and hugging Aunt Lureen and gazing up wide-eyed at Dieter, who raised his right hand for a high-five. Hey, Dieter.

Hey, buddy. How's a little fried perch sound?

Mmmmm. It was one of Hunter's favorites.

I brought you something, too, Dieter added. I'll be right back. He went out to his truck and returned a minute later with a paper bag. Go ahead, big guy, open it.

Whoaaaa. Hunter's eyes lit up at the sight of a leather pouch of marbles tied, loosely, with a bright green string. A few days before, Maggie had described Hunter's newly acquired passion for marbles, a game Dieter used to play when *he* was a boy.

With a grin that wouldn't quit, Hunter balanced the marbles in the open palm of his hand while Dieter, with his photographic memory, taught him their names. Opal, he murmured, glimmer, bull's eye, blood.

After dinner, out on the back lawn, they opened the pouch and poured the marbles inside an old hula hoop and began to position them. Meanwhile Lureen lit the tiki torches while Maggie filled an ice cream maker with fresh peaches and low fat milk.

Basking in the glow of Dieter's attention to her son, Maggie considered the twists of fate that had brought the four of them to this cabin. How many unconnected events had to fall into place for a magical night like this to occur? Colt cutting up Jimmy Santiago, Dieter returning to Crooked River, Frank Paterson hiring a stranger off the street to refinish his Belgian armoires. It all seemed so strange and tenuous, and yet here they were.

After finishing the game of marbles Dieter took his leave. He thought it important that the boy understand that his motives were pure. Hunter was no doubt already aware of Dieter's affection for his mother. He might even, by now, consider him her boyfriend. But he also genuinely liked the man, and more importantly felt comfortable around him. For one thing, unlike most adults, Dieter treated him as an equal. He didn't lose the game of marbles on purpose, for instance, and then pretend that he hadn't; because pity, in any guise, was a sham. All of which meant that it would have been a mistake for Dieter to stay over. Trust was not gained in a single evening—both Dieter and the boy instinctively understood this. Ever the gentleman, he pecked Lureen on the cheek and squeezed Maggie's shoulder and thanked them both for a wonderful evening.

When he walked away, Lureen's hungry eyes followed him, step by step, out to his truck.

Easy, sis.

Honey, that boy is a genuwine peach.

As he drove back up the driveway, a sweet, dominant aroma flooded the air. Wisteria? Russian lavender? Dieter wasn't sure, but he slowed down anyway, poking his head out the window to sniff the lovely fragrance.

The first time his family vacationed in Crooked River his mother had accompanied him on a walk through town. She was in a joyous frame of mind that morning, delighted to be back in sunny Florida at the end of a bitter northern winter, a thousand miles from all that snow. Filled with energy and verve, she grabbed Dieter's hand and swept him along the shady sidewalks, pointing out sprigs of mint in an herb garden, an orange tree bulging with fruit, Russian lavender. I have never been anywhere, she cried, that smelled so good! And she was right. Even for a nine-year-old whose idea of an evocative odor was a box of popcorn at the movies, flowering hibiscus mixed with a salty breeze off the nearby harbor made for a heady brew.

In a flash, Dieter saw his mother standing at the window of their room at the Gibson gazing down at the street. While his father and his sister dressed for dinner, the boy studied the side of his mother's face, the high, proud cheekbones that bespoke a quarter strain of Cherokee blood, the slash of cherry lipstick, the penciled brows. In her yellow summer dress she seemed indescribably elegant, almost regal, the most beautiful creature he had ever seen . . .

And then they perish, he thought. His beautiful mother, his beautiful Jen. It was a sudden and unexpected mental jolt, and it rattled him badly, and he almost swerved off the road. He was not particularly superstitious but sometimes he wondered if he was cursed. The swiftness of time and the inexplicability of early death crowded his mind. Making blind connections now, he recited a line from a poem—*anything could happen / and probably would*— his buoyant mood abruptly punctured by icy apprehension, a chill northern wind.

Rolling up his window he glimpsed, once again, the serene expression on Maggie's face as she watched him play marbles with Hunter. How utterly at peace with the world she had seemed today. But what about tomorrow, and the day after, and the day after that? What would happen then?

As he approached the town his thoughts grew increasingly bleak. The future was a blank, an abyss. Would he remain in Crooked River, courting Maggie? Would he write a second book? Would he ever go home? For the last six weeks he had dismissed such concerns, determined not to dote on them. The best course of action, he had convinced himself, was to live like a Buddhist, in the moment, for today. But now it felt as if time was running out. He would have to make some essential decisions, and he would have to make them soon.

Maggie. He thought about her constantly these days, reading a bedtime story to Hunter or rowing the canoe across the pond or gathering tomatoes from her truck patch. He was bewitched, obsessed, haunted, one of those characters in a Russian novel who walks around in a lovestruck fog. When he wasn't with her he felt miserable, and when he was, he felt afraid. If he was cursed, then she was cursed too, like Jennifer.

What he wanted, what he needed, was to get high. That was all there was to it. And tomorrow, thank God, that was exactly what he was going to do.

That morning, when he'd returned to the Blue Moon to see Gene, the usually-congenial bartender had seemed irritable, ill at ease. I can't get you scag, he growled. And I don't want to, either. Capeesh?

Taken aback by Gene's combative attitude, Dieter had merely nodded.

You don't need that shit, man, nobody does. I'm sorry, but that's how I feel.

I understand.

A flicker of a glance around the tavern to make sure no one was listening, before turning back to his friend.

What I *can* get you is some Percocet.

Yeah?

Fifty tabs.

Fifty's good. Fifty's great.

This was more like it, Dieter thought. Percocet was a popular choice in Quintana Roo, too, where you could score anything; less lethal than smack but in the correct dosage, a righteous high.

Milligrams?

Seven point five.

Excellent.

With a small, sad smile, Gene accepted Dieter's grateful hand, and then held on to it a moment too long.

You sure you wanna do this, D? You really sure?

In his room at the Gibson, Dieter poured three fingers of blended whiskey into a smudged glass. He swallowed a sleeping pill and lay back on the bed, waiting for the drug to release its potion, for his muscles, and his mind, to unwind. Worry accomplished nothing. In the end, whatever was going to happen was going to happen. He would stay in Crooked River or he'd leave. He'd break up with Maggie Paterson or declare his undying love. He'd write a sequel to *Jaguar Moon* or go back home to build cabinets. It was out of his hands now. Lureen might be convinced that God had some kind of master plan, but Dieter didn't think so. Chance, or luck, or serendipity; ultimately a random throw of the cosmic dice is what determined your fate. Ask a gambler. Ask a soldier. Ask him.

30

Raul parked his car beneath the catalpa trees behind the abandoned building. Trying to stay calm, he listened in the sudden rural silence to the tick of the Toyota's cooling engine followed, seconds later, by a ripple of wind. Checked his wristwatch, 6:45. Fifteen minutes to go, fifteen more jittery minutes until the target, expecting nothing more than a simple drug exchange, arrived. For reassurance he slipped a hand into the pocket of his windbreaker to make sure the plastic vial, as well as the pistol, was still there.

He had a bad feeling about this one. Nothing specific, nothing he could really put his finger on, just a vague unease, a roiling in his belly that made it impossible to digest the tamales he had eaten for lunch that day.

The details of the job were not the issue. The location was ideal, a neglected shack that used to house a canoe outpost on a narrow stretch of the Wakulla River five miles north of town. Empty for years, the outpost had been built in a clearing of tangled woods off a quiet country road. Out back, above the river, on a slope that was mostly weeds now, there was a rusty rack that once held the canoes, and a cedar picnic table stained gray by time.

The identity of the man he was going to kill wasn't a problem either. He was anonymous, an unknown, not even a name, and that was the way Raul preferred it. A white male in his late twenties— that was the only information he had been given, and it was all he wanted to know.

The weapon was a snub nose .38 that fit snugly in the pocket of his windbreaker. And the setup was simple. A drug deal out here in the boonies far away from curious eyes. When the target arrived, Raul would place the vial of pills on the picnic table, and when the man reached out to grab it he would shoot him between the eyes. Then he'd scatter the pills on the ground and wipe his prints off the vial and toss it down into the weeds next to the body. Simple, clean, efficient; a drug deal gone awry. And yet despite all that, he still felt queasy. Unwilling to admit that the root of his unease was a troubled conscience, he blamed it on the tamales.

He had killed twice before, the first time in Guadalajara, the year he turned seventeen. Saturday night, a deserted parking lot, two rival gangs. By prior agreement the only weapons were to be fists. But when one of the opponents, a good-looking kid who bore a striking resemblance to the actor Sal Mineo, reached into his pocket and pulled out a switchblade after Raul broke his nose with a sudden right hook, Raul reacted the only way he knew how, *al tú por tú*, unsheathing his own six-inch blade and slashing it at his assailant. The boy feinted once, twice, slicing the air and forcing Raul to back away. But on the third feint Raul was ready for him, and without giving it another thought he lashed out, driving his knife deep into the victim's ribcage. The blade severed an artery and a geyser of blood spattered the pavement as the boy collapsed. For a few minutes Raul stood over the body unable to assimilate what had just occurred. In front of his eyes, the Sal Mineo look-alike bled out, and the other fighters fled. Eventually, Raul ran also.

The second killing was preordained, strictly for cash. On an unusually chilly October evening he had waited at the end of a fishing pier on a freshwater lake in southern Alabama. He was scared and cold and impatient, stomping his boots on the pier's balky planks until headlights swept the leafy darkness and a middle-aged man Raul had never seen before climbed out of his car. The man was wearing a herringbone suit jacket, custom fit blue jeans, and black wingtips that must have been recently polished, the way they gleamed in the light of the moon. He was carrying a briefcase Raul had been instructed not to open. Whipping out his pistol, Raul waved the briefcase away and ordered the man to kneel down, facing in the opposite direction.

Afterwards, grabbing the briefcase, he marched to the end of the pier, his heart hammering so loudly he thought it was going to burst. He kept reminding himself that this was nothing more than a business transaction, but that night, and for many nights after, he woke in a cold sweat picturing, again and again, those shiny black shoes.

Sometimes he conducted imaginary conversations with the kid he'd killed in Guadalajara. Over and over he begged forgiveness until the boy, with a ghostly smile, granted his wish. But what kind of man murders a stranger for money? He could blame the killing in Guadalajara on self-defense, but in Alabama there was no such excuse. Clutching the briefcase, he had hurried down the pier wondering how he was going to live with himself now.

Kill once on contract and you establish a street rep and inevitably, other offers come your way. And yet for the last seven years, ever since that dreadful night in Alabama, Raul had rejected every one. The money was enticing but there was more to life, he had discovered, than a bank account. For one, there was Marlena to think about, Marlena and their three adorable kids.

After moving to Crooked River he had lived, for a time, within his means, slaving five days a week on a roofing crew sloshing hot black tar. It was tough, mindless labor but the paychecks were steady and there was usually a little left over at the end of the month. When Marlena returned to work at Ochoas following the birth of their third (and last, they decided) child, there was even a little more. With two paychecks coming in every week they felt flush enough to put a down payment on a two-bedroom home. In addition they purchased, on installment, a dishwasher for Marlena, a swing set for the kids, and new furniture. To a poor immigrant like Raul it was the American dream, deficit spending providing a predictable life with modest rewards he and Marlena learned to cherish. A baby's first steps, a three-day vacation at a motel on Clearwater Beach, a report card featuring one or two A's.

Raul tried not to dote on the mountain of debt they seemed to have abruptly accumulated (he wasn't sure what a balloon mortgage was, but apparently they had one) or how, when the dust finally settled, they would possibly pay it off. And then one fateful Sunday evening a local bookie strolled into the bar at Ochoas and talked Raul into placing a side bet on the baseball game he was watching on TV. Raul won the bet and collected the stranger's twenty, and all at once he saw a way to scramble out of the financial hole he had tumbled into. All he needed was a bit of luck.

It didn't take long for Raul to become one of the bookie's steadiest customers. Baseball, jai alai, the dog races at Derby Lane, the yearly pigskin rivalry between Florida and Florida State; after awhile it didn't really matter *what* he bet on because the real payoff was the juice, the buzz, the willingness to take risks.

For a time he did okay, too, losing now and then but in the end at worst breaking even. Then his luck ran dry and he had no choice but to cover one bet with another, robbing Peter to pay Paul. The vig alone was killing him, so he started to do a little freelance work on the side for the bookie and some of his friends. Not breaking kneecaps—that was Hollywood's version— but nonetheless convincing poor suckers just like him to fork over their life savings or suffer the consequences of saying no. Sometimes he wore brass knuckles, or carried a gun, and yet he continued to draw the line at killing. Right up, that is, until now.

A few days ago when Colt Taylor requested a meeting, Jimmy Santiago had suggested the bar at Ochoas. On the appointed evening, Marlena posted a Closed sign on the front door, dimmed the overhead lights and placed, on the table where the men were waiting, a bottle of tequila and three cans of beer.

The tension was intense. Jimmy, for one, remained adamantly silent while refusing, when Colt lifted his shot glass for a mutual toast, to acknowledge the gesture. In response, Colt merely shrugged, unwilling to let the slight deter him. In a quiet, measured voice he apologized to Jimmy for cutting him at the club. Then he turned to Raul.

A man has to pay for his mistakes. I understand that now.

Raul waited for more. An eye for an eye, Colt added. I believe in that, too.

Raul flicked a glance at Jimmy, whose impassive expression gave nothing away.

So this is why you called the meeting?

To let it go.

To let it go? The gold tooth, the menacing smile. *No comprendo, señor.*

To move on.

Ah, to move on. *Sí.* There was more to this, then. Raul raised his shot glass. So let us move on, *amigo.* Please. Continue.

To show good faith, Colt wanted to offer them a deal.

Jimmy, who had yet to utter a word, finally leaned in toward the man he had once considered a *compañero.* A deal?

A contract.

Raul was confused. All along he had been expecting a double cross but this didn't sound like one. Colt Taylor was a tough guy, maybe even stand up in a funny sort of way—he hadn't, after all, blown the whistle after the beating out on Pheasant Hill Road— but he was no mover and shaker like his boss Teddy Mink, and Raul had a hard time believing he could come up with something this elaborate as the basis for a betrayal. With rising interest he listened to Colt describe the canoe outpost, the Percocet, the gun.

And the target, *señor?*

A white male, Colt replied, in his late twenties. Nothing else. Not the man's name nor his occupation nor what he had done to deserve such a fate.

The figure was fifteen hundred dollars, a sum Colt agreed, at Jimmy's insistence, to provide upfront. Meekly, the mule gazed down at the floor. Look, I'd do this myself but I don't . . .

What? You don't what? Raul demanded.

Have the balls. Colt forced himself to look across the table at Raul. I've never done anything like that before.

This surprising confession of macho weakness convinced Raul that Colt wasn't lying. Teddy Mink—who else could it be?— wanted someone dead, and he was willing to pay for it. Besides, by asking for the money upfront, Jimmy had exposed Colt's hand and taken a double cross out of the equation. Then Raul recalled the shiny black wingtips the man he had murdered in Alabama was wearing that night and all at once he felt ill. Despite his vow never to kill again, he knew he was going to cave. It was as simple as that; he was going to buckle. Your move, *amigo.*

Okay then. Colt reached into his wallet and counted out, one by one, fifteen bills.

Behind the canoe outpost Raul checked his wristwatch again. Less than five minutes to go. To work off some of his nervous energy he climbed out of the car and walked over to the shack and peeked inside. Nothing. An empty room, walls stained black with mildew, broken panes. Still antsy, he ambled over to the river to watch the tea-colored current carry sticks and leaves downstream. Then he heard the toot of a horn and wheeled around in time to see a blue pickup ease into the drive.

Dieter was not particularly surprised to see Raul waiting for him under the catalpas. Gene had told him that a man—he wasn't sure who—would meet him at the outpost to exchange the drugs. So why shouldn't that man be someone with real street savvy, Dieter thought, like his friend Raul?

But if Dieter wasn't particularly surprised to see Raul, the hit man was flabbergasted. His mind refused to accept what his eyes were telling him was true. He recalled Colt's brief description of the victim—*a white male in his late twenties*—and tried to match that description to the man standing in front of him now, but his mind balked. No, this had to be some kind of mistake, some kind of misunderstanding.

Buenas noches, amigo! Sliding out of his truck, Dieter raised a hand in greeting. Then he noticed the blank look on his friend's face.

Buenas noches, Raul mechanically replied.

Something was wrong. Dieter could feel it, the bad vibes. People thought that phrase was silly and outdated but it wasn't; sometimes there was a shimmer of evil in the air. He glanced around the weedy clearing to see if anyone else was there. Because something was definitely wrong. Raul, who under any other circumstances would have greeted his gringo friend with lively banter and a gleaming gold tooth, was eerily silent today. And his eyes were unsteady, shifting back and forth.

As Dieter stepped across the clearing Raul reached into the pocket of his windbreaker and withdrew a vial of yellow pills.

Dieter hesitated, looking down at the vial. So that's it, he said lamely. Percocet, *sí?*

Sí, senor. Not taking his eyes off the target, Raul placed the vial on the table. Percocet. What you requested, no?

Why, Dieter wondered, is he being so formal? This was a man he had broken bread with. He knew his wife, his children, considered him a friend. He couldn't comprehend what was happening. In disbelief he watched Raul slip a hand into the pocket of his windbreaker again and this time withdraw a gun.

Dieter stared at the pistol without comprehension, like a man in shock. Why was his friend pointing a gun at him? He had just come here to buy some pills.

Raul, *amigo, que esta pasado?*

In lieu of an answer Raul went into a crouch, which in Dieter's fragmented state of mind seemed almost comical, a bad actor's unconvincing performance in a movie no one would ever see. Gripping the .38 in both of his stubby hands, the hit man circled his quarry, until he was standing directly behind him.

Dieter swiveled his head, trying to see what Raul was doing. It occurred to him that this must be a scam, a joke. Was that it? Was this some kind of elaborate practical joke? He had seen Raul's playful side before, goofing around with his bambinos. Would he turn around now and discover the pistol was a toy, the whole charade some kind of elaborate bluff?

But the answer was no. Raul's sad, raspy voice issued a command and in that surreal moment Dieter knew that this was no ruse. The man was going to rob him, perhaps even kill him. But why?

Arrodillese, amigo. Arrodillese ahorita por favor. Dieter could hear the sorrow in Raul's voice, and the strain. In a daze, he obeyed, kneeling down in the ragged weeds. This is it, he thought. For some reason I'm to die beside a river in Florida. He closed his eyes, waiting for the bullet, and saw his father in his workshop, Maggie in her kitchen, Jen on the beach in Quintana Roo . . .

He heard Raul begin to murmur a Spanish prayer. Then he felt the barrel of the pistol press against the back of his head as it began to rain, a spatter of drops dimpling the river and tapping the leaves of the trees. Addled by terror, he deemed this somehow appropriate; to die in the rain, as Jen had. His mind detached from his body and he floated up through the damp air until he was high enough to gaze back down, with some dispassion, at the clearing where his double knelt in the shadow of his assassin. Soon it would be over. He closed his eyes, took a final breath, and repeated, word for word, the Spanish prayer Raul kept reciting as he'd squeezed the trigger, flung the gun into the river, and fled.

31

After a ringing telephone at 3:00 a.m. left him with no choice but to lie in the dark listening to jittery Gene whine like a little girl about the contract to kill William Dieter, Colt had been unable to go back to sleep. He fidgeted with the sheets, punched the inadequate pillow, tried in vain to ignore the lighted numbers on Nicky Meyers's bedside clock. In the past, visualizing certain successful golf shots had sometimes conquered his insomnia, so he tried that too, replaying the first four holes at Hopkins Creek, which he had maneuvered around last week at one under par. But even the epic tee shot on the opening hole or that twisty downhill putt, a double breaker, on the par-three fourth failed to lull him back to sleep, so he finally gave up. He climbed out of bed and stomped into the kitchen and switched on the overhead lights. Fuck it. If he was going to be up all night he may as well get a buzz on. He yanked open the fridge and fished out a bottle of beer.

A what? When Gene breathed into the phone Colt swore he could smell the cheap bourbon on the bartender's sour breath.

A premonition.

Great. So you're what's his name now, that psychic.

Wait. I guess it was more like a dream.

Go figure, Colt moaned, glancing at the bedside clock. I mean it's only three in the morning, right?

Gene ignored the jab. In the dream, he said, Dieter's motives were pure. He was staying in town because he was writing a book about it.

A book.

Yeah, a book, about Crooked River. He *is* a writer you know.

Was, Colt thought, *was* a writer.

The rest of it, Gene spat, is bullshit, Teddy's paranoia.

Colt was losing his patience. Before Gene so rudely awakened him he had been dreaming about Anita Ekberg tooling around Rome on the back of a scooter driven by you know who. Flashing cameras, honking car horns, a pack of fans gawking at the famous starlet and her new handsome friend.

Look, it wasn't *my* idea.

What wasn't?

The contract!

Doesn't matter, *you* set it up.

Colt's anger, held in check so far, flared. Now hold on. Let's get this story straight, huh. I mean there wouldn't even be any contract if you didn't, you know . . .

Didn't what?

Egg Teddy on. Feed his paranoia.

Colt imagined the pained expression on the bartender's face: shock, outrage, despair.

You're missing the point.

Am I?

Damn right.

Which is what, Gene? Why don't you go ahead and tell me the point.

The point is he's innocent. Gene waited for this simple revelation to sink in. Got that? Innocent.

Colt had had enough. Fuck you want *me* to do about it?

Call it off.

I can't, Colt growled. It's too late. It's already over.

After a long pause Gene's voice returned, deflated this time. I can't believe this, man. I can't believe it.

Get some sleep, Geno. Stop worrying so much. It'll all look better to you in the morning.

And yet sleep, Colt suspected, was no more likely for the troubled bartender tonight than it was for him. In Nicky Meyers's tiny kitchen—not that she needed a bigger one, not that she ever actually cooked—he sat down at the breakfast table and chugged the rest of his beer. He thought about the bag of coke he had stashed a couple weeks ago in the back of Nicky's pantry. One of his cardinal rules was to never get high the night before a job, but this was no ordinary run, so the rules, he decided, didn't apply. He opened a second bottle of Bud, weighing his options. He could chill out with a few cold brews and then try, once more, to go back to sleep, or he could hoover a line or two and get ready—hell, it was already three-thirty, right?—for the big day. Hangovers played hell on his nerves but if he paced himself he would be all right.

In the living room he settled into one of Nicky's wing chairs and switched on the TV, even though the images, in the wake of the first explosive line of coke, failed to hold his attention for very long. Unfortunately Gene's whiny voice came needling its way back into his conscience. Why didn't the dumb fuck take a sleeping pill and keep his worries to himself? Talk about *Teddy's* paranoia. He loved Gene like a brother but prison had taken something out of the man; his edge, his nerve, his chutzpah.

With a razor blade and a hand mirror, Colt divided a second line, a modest little bump to keep the juices flowing. The key was to space the bumps out more or less evenly and thus control the trajectory of your high. Scrape the line, roll the dollar bill, bend over the hand mirror and say ahhhhh . . . Rapture, ecstasy, bliss.

Thank God Nicky had driven up to Macon to visit her ailing mother tonight. Because the last thing he needed right now was a bimbo with nothing better to do flitting around the apartment wondering why, as long as he was shacking up in her pad, he didn't fork over half of the rent. It was almost as if Nicky was hoping that her nagging would make him leave, not realizing that this was precisely what he was planning to do. It was comical, really, the way she kept harassing him about a little rent money right before he hit the jackpot, mere days before his ship sailed in. Everywhere you went these days someone put the squeeze on. Oh well. When he got down to Mexico he'd send the stripper a chipper little note—thanks for the mammaries, babe—just to let her know there were no hard feelings.

On TV a woman bearing an unfortunate resemblance to Tammy Faye Baker was attempting to sell insomniacs like Colt bizarre kitchen gadgets they couldn't possibly have a use for. A salad shooter? What the fuck was a salad shooter? In disgust he grabbed the remote and shut it off. There was a lot on his mind and he didn't need any more distractions tonight. A lot on his mind . . . like the fact that tomorrow was the most important day of the rest of his life, the fork in the crooked road that would eventually lead to a villa in Mexico overlooking the turquoise sea. He leaned over and inhaled line number three, feeling the blast in the back of his throat and the sockets of his eyes simultaneously. A crooked smile confirmed his growing optimism, the world through coke-colored glasses. In Sarasota, Eddie would cut the batch by a third, upping the ante because that's the way it was done these days. The buyers wouldn't expect anything else, and besides, they would step on it too. It was the law of diminishing returns. By the time the stuff hit the streets it would be a little bit of coke and a whole lot of baking powder sailing right up the noses of all those chumps who thought they were buying the real thing. Fuck 'em—that's what you got for living in Philadelphia.

When his heartbeat slowed down to a reasonable stutter he went into the bathroom and turned the shower on high, adjusting Nicky's massage nozzle until the stinging needles of water were transformed into a warm, pulsing spray. And fifteen minutes later he was ready for the day, showered and shaved and dressed in the kind of nondescript clothing—blue jeans and a plain gray T-shirt—he liked to wear on runs. For a drug mule, anonymity was a must.

In the parking lot of Nicky's apartment complex he placed his valise—which contained what was left of the coke, a pint of Wild Turkey, and the .45 he always carried with him on runs—in the trunk of his car alongside the suitcase he had packed the night before. In no particularly hurry, he cruised down Cypress Avenue toward Highway 98 then swung north toward Panama City, where he signed the agreement for the rental, a black Trans Am this time, in the office of the usual lot.

Adjusting the Trans Am's mirrors, he circled back south to pick up the goods. For October it was an unseasonably humid day, and at the bottom of shallow concavities in the highway, mirages of water appeared. Orange groves, flat-water rivers, deep piney woods. Colt had always considered this a particularly scenic and unspoiled stretch of road, but he took little pleasure in it today. The trouble was that he was starting to crash, and he hadn't had anything to eat yet either, a lethal combination. The only answer he could come up with was another bump, so he pulled into a rest stop and parked in the far corner of the lot, in the shade of a gnarled old oak. On the dash he divided a hefty line with the edge of a credit card, snorted the powder with a five-dollar bill, and chased it with a slug of Wild Turkey.

There, that was better. Just what the doctor ordered. What a morning! As he pulled back onto the highway his spirits soared, and why not? The engine of the Trans Am hummed like a spaceship, the sun shimmered on the Apalachicola River, and that new song by Dire Straits—the one with the kickass riff— was blasting from the box. Best of all, the day of Teddy Mink's comeuppance had finally arrived. How sweet revenge tasted when you had waited this long.

With an eye on the speedometer—a speeding ticket at this point was not an option—he gathered his thoughts. Okay, so the timing of the hit had been terrible, and as far as he could determine the contract had been unwarranted. There was little doubt that Dieter, as Gene suggested, was an innocent man. Morally this was reprehensible, a genuine downer. And yet now that Dieter was out of the way Colt's path back to Maggie looked a lot less cluttered than before. When he saw her today he would offer his condolences, or if the body hadn't been discovered yet, quietly explain that he was going away. Mexico, he would confide, a little village on the west coast. Perhaps in a few weeks she and Hunter could fly over for a visit, at Colt's expense. No strings attached, he would assure her, just some down time in the sun on Hunter's Thanksgiving break. All he had to do was plant the seed. In the darkness of her grief the flower would blossom, because even a woman as tough as Maggie craved unconditional love, and with Dieter out of the picture Colt was the only man who could offer her that. The father of her child, the partner she had lived with for the last five years, the man who knew her better than anyone else. Hell, if she played her cards right who knew, he might even marry her!

Bearing south, he went over the blueprint again. After picking up the shipment at the airstrip he would stop by Maggie's cabin for a quick goodbye. Then he'd head down the coast. Concluding that Pam Morgan was no longer reliable, Teddy had switched the safe house from Everglades City to some old cracker shack at the end of a deserted lane near Clearwater Beach, and at first Colt had been thrown for a loop by this change in his itinerary. Then he'd realized that the proximity of the new safe house would buy him a little more time. Even with a late start he could make it to Clearwater by early evening. And the following morning, after a good night's rest, he could cruise on down to Sarasota, meet the buyers, and board a red eye to Puerto Vallarta that very same night.

The plan was ingenious, foolproof, a template of righteous revenge. At last Teddy Mink would pay for his sins, for humiliating him in front of Nicky Meyers, and for trotting out the dead father, proving that he was the biggest prick of all. Colt's only regret was that he wouldn't be there to see the bewildered expression on the kingpin's face when he realized what his lowly mule had just done.

To celebrate his good fortune, he swung off the highway onto an old logging road that wound back through a tunnel of trees. There wasn't much to look at—a murky pond, some abandoned bee boxes, and a glimpse, here and there, of a patch of blue sky— but the view didn't matter. He pulled into a clearing in the woods to divide two more lines on the dashboard. Glancing in the rear view mirror, he hoovered both lines, chasing each one with a generous gulp of Wild Turkey. Soon the bottle was empty, and so was the bag, but that didn't matter either, for Colt was oblivious now. His eyes were closed. His mind was at rest. He was dreaming about Mexico.

32

At dawn Dieter woke in the crushed weeds, somehow still breathing. Cocking open one eye he observed on the bed of wet leaves which had cushioned his fall a stain darker than the rain, a ribbon of blood, his. Then he drifted off, and when he woke again the bizarre notion that somehow at point blank range Raul had missed him flickered through his mind. Randomly he began to mutter the lyrics of a song he'd recently heard on the radio—something by Joni Mitchell—a man in shock or on the verge of delirium astonished to discover that he was still there. Or was he? Had he woken in the real world or were these the final earthly visions of someone who had already died? Was he lying in the clearing with a bullet in his brain? If so, he would enter the land of the dead now, purged, purified, saved.

Shivering in the damp and cold, he recalled the first step of that purification, how he had floated up out of his body to gaze back down at the nightmare tableau the instant Raul fired his gun. But wait. How could a dead man remember the sound of the gunshot that killed him? And how could Raul, a marksman, miss his target at point blank range? No, neither of those scenarios was even remotely plausible. In a panic, Raul must have fired out over the river or up into the trees. At the penultimate moment, the assassin's nerves had presumably failed. Lashing out at his own inadequacy, he must have then cold-cocked his victim with the barrel of the pistol, which would explain both the blackout Dieter was now rousing from, as well as the painful gash in the back of his head.

Later he woke to another dream; birdsong in the branches and the steady flow of the River Styx, his final passage. And yet that wasn't plausible either, because no boatman waited at the ferry and Dieter, against odds, was still alive. With great care he pressed his palms against the bloody leaves, trying to lift his upper body, until a jolt of electricity hammered him back to the ground. Delicately, he probed the head wound and his fingers came away sticky. Swallowing the bile in his throat, he braced himself for what he had to do. The knowledge that he was still losing blood deepened his resolve, and by pressing his hands against the ground again and ignoring what felt like a drill boring into the back of his skull he was finally able to struggle to his feet, woozy as a newborn colt. He stared in wonder at the river, as if seeing water for the very first time.

As the light broke through the boughs of the catalpas and streamed across the clearing, he staggered over to his truck. Inside the cab he found keys in the ignition and his wallet on the front seat. Cash, credit cards, driver's license, photograph of Jen; nothing, it appeared, was missing.

Once more his tentative fingers probed, through matted hair, the open wound. Determined to staunch the flow of blood, he slipped off his T-shirt and tore it into rags and with one of the strips bound the gash in a headband. Catching sight of himself in the driver's window, he thought about the young soldier in *The Red Badge of Courage* wrapping his own head wound in a similar fashion. Like Raul, the boy soldier had fled, horrified by what he had been commanded to do.

On the bank of the river he washed his face and his chest with a cup of two hands. Loosening the headband, he rinsed this in the river also, and when the rag was wrung dry, or at least damp, retied it. His mind wandered back and forth through time, disengaged. In Quintana Roo, Parrish wore his bandanna as a sweatband, just as he had in Vietnam; because the Mekong Delta, even in Mexico, was never far away. Every jungle, he told Dieter one night, is the same. The only difference here is that the bullets are imaginary, at least so far.

He climbed into the pickup and turned the key in the ignition and crawled down the weedy drive. Now that the initial elation of survival had begun to wear off, he took stock of his situation. Yes, he was alive, all right, but someone was trying to kill him and he couldn't fathom why. If the motive was robbery, why was his wallet still there? And if it wasn't robbery, what other reason could there be? He dismissed the possibility that the plan had originated with Raul. Based on the hit man's startled expression when his target pulled into the outpost, it seemed likely that he hadn't even been told the identity of the man he was supposed to kill. He wracked his brain for possible enemies, and came up blank. Since he had arrived in Crooked River he had made only friends: Maggie, Frank Paterson, the deckhands, Lureen, Consuela, Mr. Gold. With every one of them he had behaved like the gentleman he considered himself to be.

And then an altogether different face flashed through his mind, and all at once he knew, without a doubt, who had ordered the killing.

On Pheasant Hill Road he pulled into the parking lot of a convenience store with an Open sign shining in its murky window. Inside, a teenaged girl with straight brown hair parted down the middle stood behind the counter tracking the disheveled stranger now climbing, gingerly, out of his truck. Narrowing her eyes, she watched him hesitate in the doorway.

Morning.

Morning, she squeaked. Can I help you?

Grimacing—the least movement was still agony—he shook

his head. No, he lied, I'm fine. I'm just fine.

Considering what he must look like to her—a bare-chested madman with a bloody rag wrapped around his head—Dieter was hardly surprised by the glint of fear in the girl's eyes, but there was nothing he could do about that. Determined to get in and out of the store as quickly as possible, he worked his way down one of the garish aisles, baffled by the sheer volume of junk food—candy, cookies, chips—dominating the entire row. He imagined a rabble of children swarming through the store after school grabbing this package and that. Halfway down the aisle these random, disconnected thoughts caused him to pause, suddenly disoriented, suddenly off task, unable to remember why he was there.

The clerk was watching his every move. He was a handsome guy but who came to a convenience store on a Friday morning without a shirt on? And what about the headband? Was that red stain seeping out of it blood? The man frightened her, and yet when he turned back to the counter he looked so confused and forlorn she felt a stab of pity, too.

Band-aids? Dieter lifted his hands in a gesture of helplessness. Bandages?

She pointed a shaky finger. Right behind you.

Of course, he cried. Another grimace: his voice was too loud, too demonstrative. He had to tone it down before she called the cops, triggered an alarm, dashed out of the store. Mouthing thanks, he filled his arms with a box of bandages, a bottle of peroxide, and a vial of Tylenol, and carried them over to the counter.

The clerk rang up his purchases and stuffed them into a plastic bag. Then a cloud drifted across the room . . . and Dieter was lost again. As Raul pressed the barrel of the pistol against the back of his head he heard the cry of a hawk in the mist above the river. A night hawk? A kestrel? Jen would have known. She would have pointed to the appropriate panel in Petersen's Guide. Meanwhile a sudden flurry of rain spattered the tannic river.

You all right, mister? A flurry of rain spattered the river while

Raul, already in mourning, recited a passage of prayer. Mister?

Yeah?

You okay?

That all depends, he thought, on how you define okay. He pursed his lips. He wanted to ease the clerk's anxiety but he didn't know how to accomplish that. She thought he was crazy, and maybe she was right. Maybe the episode in the clearing had unhinged his mind. What, he wondered, would madness look like? A clearing in the woods? A river in the rain?

Well are you?

Am I what?

Okay?

Without warning, her innocent question unleashed a flood of emotions and tears glistened in his eyes and he had to grab on to the edge of the counter for balance.

Look, I'm sorry if I scared you, barging in like this. I didn't mean to do that.

Fractionally, the clerk's expression softened. Apparently his apology had muted, to some degree, her apprehension. That's all right, she said. Job like this, you see all kinds!

I was in an accident.

I can see that.

By the river.

The Wakulla?

Yeah, that one.

The girl twirled a strand of her hair. Do you want me to call someone for help? I can do that you know.

Dieter took a closer look at her. Her skin was clear and her eyes were blue and when she smiled her heartbreaking little smile there was a glimmer of metal braces. She reminded him of a girl in a painting by Vermeer, sad and vulnerable and terribly needy, the kind of young woman who would be hurt, over and over, by men. Stifling an urge to reach out and press her against his chest while he described what it felt like to kneel down in a weedy clearing and glimpse nothingness, he scattered some bills on the counter, mumbled another apology, and staggered out of the store.

~

Maggie was brewing a second pot of coffee—she had just driven Hunter, who had missed the bus, to school—when Dieter's truck fishtailed down the drive. At the sight of the bloody rag she raced out the door.

My God, Dieter, what happened to you? She helped him out of the truck and ushered him into the kitchen. The fuck happened? Who *did* this?

Later it would all come back to him: the flat light in the kitchen, a wall calendar featuring a photograph of flamingos, Maggie's faint, windy voice.

You stay right there. Opening the door underneath the sink, she grabbed a handful of rags and a metal basin. At the stove, she heated a kettle of water.

Lean your head down, there, like that. With a rag dipped in the warm basin she cleaned, as best she could, the gash Raul's pistol had torn open. The hair around it was stiff with dried blood. Out in the truck, he groaned. There's some bandages, some peroxide.

Returning to the kitchen, Maggie wet a second rag with the peroxide and gently pressed it against the wound, biting her lip in sympathy every time Dieter flinched.

Hold on, hon, this won't take long.

She waited for the peroxide to bubble before dabbing the wound dry. Then she applied, with the detached efficiency of a nurse who had done this a thousand times before, a fresh bandage.

There.

Inch by inch he lifted his head, gauging the level of pain. Coffee, he croaked. Could you bring me some coffee?

With his hands wrapped around the cup, Dieter told her about the Percocet, the meeting by the river, Raul's gun.

Maggie was confused, angry, and frightened. The men she loved kept showing up on her doorstep in disrepair.

But why would Raul try to kill you? I thought he was your friend.

He *is* my friend.

Some friend!

Look, I don't think it was his idea. I don't even think he knew who he was supposed to kill.

In the ensuing silence they listened to the tick of the clock on the kitchen wall count off each uneasy second. The implications of Dieter's statement had stalled the conversation, but sooner or later one of them had to speak.

What are you saying, Dieter?

It was too late to mince words, to make excuses. They had to face the truth. I'm saying that someone hired him.

Someone? Maggie hung her head, sickened by the realization that Dieter meant Colt, and that he was probably right. Abruptly she scooted her chair back and stood up to check the bandage. Already a faint pink blush was starting to seep through.

You're gonna need stitches.

I don't think so.

And we better call the cops.

Not yet. All at once, sitting there in that warm, sun-filled room, he was overcome by fatigue. Please. I need to rest first.

Unable to deny this simple request, Maggie ushered him back to the bedroom and turned down the sheets, wrapping an old towel around the pillow to protect it. When he woke a few hours later she cleaned and dressed the wound again, encouraged by the lack of fresh blood on the bandage. Head wounds, she recalled, tended to close fairly quickly if they weren't too deep.

In the closet she found a checkered shirt Colt had left at the house. She laid the shirt down on the bed next to his khaki pants, which she had washed while he was sleeping. Then she went into the kitchen and heated up two bowls of soup for their lunch.

When they finished eating, Maggie refilled their coffee

cups and for a time they sat at the kitchen table in silence again, avoiding the one subject they both knew they would have to confront. When he finds out Raul didn't do it, Maggie finally whispered, he'll come after you himself.

As if fearful that someone might be eavesdropping, Dieter lowered his voice too. I don't think so. I don't think he has the nerve. That's why he hired Raul.

We have to call the cops.

Just stay calm. He reached across the table to squeeze her hands. They felt cold and dry, like parchment. We'll get through this. I promise.

In exasperation, Maggie jerked her hands away. You're trying to protect him, aren't you?

Protect who?

Raul!

I don't know. Dieter hung his head, refusing to meet her eyes. I don't know what I'm trying to do.

When Hunter came home Maggie ran out to the front yard to warn him that Dieter had been in an accident and didn't look too good. She saw a shadow pass across the boy's face and she knew that he was thinking about his father lying in bed a few weeks ago swaddled in similar bandages. A flesh wound, she said, to counter his fear. Nothing to worry about, 'kay?

'Kay.

To prove that Maggie wasn't lying, Dieter stood up when the boy entered the kitchen and announced that this was as good a time as any for him and Hunter to go out to the pond and catch a couple perch.

For supper?

That's right, big guy, for supper.

Yay!

Dieter knelt down until his face was level with the boy's. And if we ask real nice—he gave Hunter a confidential wink—I bet your mother'd make us some peach cobbler.

In the kitchen, Maggie watched Hunter cast his line into the shallows, standing next to Dieter just as he used to stand next to his dad. She felt a pang of regret over the way she was raising her child, even though she knew the circumstances which kept disrupting his life were not her fault. Regardless, she felt bad for him, considering how much he missed Colt. Then she heard a squeal of joy and glanced out the window again as Hunter lifted a fat silver perch out of the water.

The boy started to turn toward the cabin to show his mother the perch but something distracted him. Tingling with sudden fear, Maggie followed Hunter's nervous gaze as it swung out toward the black Trans Am skidding to a stop in the gravel drive.

She immediately picked up the phone and called the local precinct. A patrolman, the dispatcher assured her, was on his way.

As she put down the phone, an egret rose up from the shallows and soared across the pond. Momentarily dazzled, Maggie watched the flight of the snow-white bird against the wall of dark trees on the opposite shore. Then her attention was drawn back to the driveway, back to Colt, who was stumbling across the gravel with a pistol in his hand.

33

On Friday afternoon police officer Dave Kershaw, the same patrolman who had found Colt Taylor cut and bleeding out on Pheasant Hill Road six weeks before, responded to a report of a domestic disturbance at Maggie Paterson's cabin. Minutes later, when he arrived at the location, officer Kershaw noted three other vehicles parked on the property: a jeep directly behind the cabin, a blue Ford pickup in the driveway, and next to the truck, a black Trans Am. Parking his own cruiser facing the pond so that he could crouch behind the hood, if necessary, while keeping the cabin in his direct line of sight, Kershaw also took note of the four people gathered, like figures in a painting, on the dock and the lawn.

Instantly he was able to identify three of them: Maggie Paterson, who had paused in mid-step halfway across the yard when she spotted the cruiser; Colt Taylor, who was striding toward the dock; and the boy, Hunter. The fourth figure, the young man with the pageboy haircut standing on the dock next to Hunter, was a stranger.

What officer Kershaw couldn't have known was that in Colt

Taylor's drug-addled mind the man on the dock wasn't a stranger but a ghost. Because William Dieter was dead, lying in the bloody weeds behind a canoe outpost. So how could he be here, Colt wondered, here at the cabin, fishing with his boy?

He had climbed out of the Trans Am without the faintest idea of his intentions. There was a gun in his right hand but he didn't know what it was doing there, and he had no recollection of retrieving it from the glove compartment of the car. He wasn't sure what he was supposed to do now, either, though it seemed imperative he at least go over to the dock and ask the ghost some questions. Like why he was wearing his shirt, and why he was fishing with his son, and why, for that matter, he had risen from the dead. Then he heard Maggie's cry from the far side of the lawn and at the same time, out of the corner of his eye, saw a police cruiser pull up next to his car.

Instinctively Dieter wrapped an arm around the boy's shoulder, pressing him to his side. Maggie paused in mid-stride. And officer Kershaw, who had not had a chance to call for backup, crouched behind the hood of the cruiser gripping, in both of his shaky hands, his own weapon.

It occurred to Colt that perhaps he should take this opportunity to inform the police officer that his .45 was fully registered and that as a long-time resident of Crooked River, and the son of a local cop, he had every right to carry it on his person. But the policeman preempted him.

Freeze!

Kershaw, Colt thought. Wait a minute, I *know* this guy.

Put down your weapon!

The day after his father's funeral half a dozen fellow police officers, including patrolman Kershaw, had stopped by the Taylor house to offer their condolences to Colt and his mom. Their intent was to assure them that officer Taylor had acted both professionally and honorably, and that the shooting of Tina Johnson was a tragic accident no one could have prevented.

Freeze! Colt tried to focus. Cattails swayed in the breeze at the edge of the pond but no, he would not dive into them at the last moment. If he did, the bullet meant for him would strike Hunter instead, just as his dad's had struck Tina Johnson.

Colt? Startled by the sound of Maggie's voice he wheeled around. She was standing on the lawn not ten feet away and there were tears in her eyes but something in her voice, too, akin to affection. Put it down, honey. Please, put it down.

He wanted to tell her how much he loved her, and how sorry he was. He wanted to tell her that everything was going to be okay.

Freeze, goddammit! PUT THE FUCKING GUN DOWN!

But I already did, Colt thought. No, wait . . . Jesse Taylor was screaming at the black man to put down his weapon. Tina Johnson was there too but Jesse couldn't see her because she was hiding behind her father.

The assailant, who was visibly agitated, Kershaw would later tell investigators, proceeded to raise his pistol. Yes, he admitted, Mr. Taylor may have been lifting his hands in surrender, but he was also holding a gun. What, he wanted to know, would *you* have done?

Colt?

The first bullet struck him in the throat, severing his jugular before exiting through the back of his neck. The second shattered his chest, puncturing the aorta.

Maggie was running across the yard. In her peripheral vision she saw Dieter lift the boy in his arms and shield him from the shooting so he couldn't see what was happening to his dad.

EPILOGUE

The first day on the road, Hunter barely spoke a word. As if drugged, he gazed dully out the window at the passing landscape, at the mist in the foothills and the gradual ascent up the mountain and the needles of the roadside conifers shivering in gusts of wind. A timbered peak then the long freefall down the opposite slope accompanied by weightlessness, vertigo. He thought about astronauts floating in space, flower petals, seeds. If you ever let go, *you* could vanish too. Souls white as snow released into the afterworld and forgotten.

On the second day Maggie followed Dieter into a gas station, urging him not to worry about the boy. When he was ready to talk, she said, he would do so. Until then, she thought it best not to press.

Assuming that Hunter's withdrawal was a delayed reaction to his father's violent death, Dieter accommodated his silence by pretending that nothing was wrong. He talked about his favorite movies, his favorite baseball team, his favorite foods. He bought the boy chili dogs and French fries, chocolate sundaes, a banana split. At night in their motel room he read him the stories of Dr. Seuss.

And then on the third morning, Hunter suddenly broke out of his shell. After a cursory glance at the breakfast menu at a roadside diner he looked up at Dieter and asked him what red-eye gravy was.

You take the drippings from a ham, Dieter replied, and mix it with black coffee.

The boy's eyes grew round as saucers. Coffee?

Listen, it's better than it sounds. You should try it.

Hunter lifted his brows and curled his lips in disbelief, as if to imply that Dieter had apparently gone mad.

I don't *think* so.

For Dieter, this unexpected exchange was like a cool wind wafting across a summer meadow, waking various birds.

I'll make you a deal. How about I get the red-eye gravy and you get the French toast. How's that sound?

They stayed in a motel outside Macon and a rooming house in Chattanooga and for three days, in a cabin in the mountains of east Tennessee. The cabin was paneled in planks of cedar that smelled like rain. There was a lake where they could fish for bluegills and a tire swing hanging from the bough of a Japanese maple. One evening Dieter found half a bottle of bourbon and a Monopoly board in a back pantry. With a mischievous grin he mixed two hefty drinks (along with a virgin cocktail for Hunter) and divvied out the fake cash. Then he rolled the dice and landed on Redding Railroad. Soon he had accumulated so many properties Maggie complained that it wasn't fair.

What's fair got to do with it?

For some reason Dieter's flip remark tripped Hunter's funny bone and he rolled around on the floor clutching a wad of colorful money. Yeah, Mom, what's fair got to do with it?

Each morning over breakfast they studied the road map before deciding where to go. The route was generally north but Dieter remained open to suggestions. Since they were in no particular hurry they avoided the interstates for county highways where they discovered roadside stands selling racks of ribs and motels featuring teepees. To give Hunter a deeper sense of complicity in the journey, Dieter showed him how to decipher the symbols on the map. Those squiggly blue lines, he said, are the rivers; the red ones are the roads.

Every other day Maggie called her father and her sister from a pay phone, allowing Hunter to chat with his grandparents, with his aunt Lureen, with Toby. She assured her father that they were all fine and that even though she didn't know when they would return he was not to fret. Naturally Frank Paterson sounded worried anyway—he couldn't understand what they were doing out there—but he did his best to keep his tone upbeat, especially when he spoke to the boy.

One afternoon, the dark skies over the hill country they were passing through opened up and showered the truck with cold rain. Hunter called the rain an "omen" though he wasn't quite sure if that was the right word. Dieter nodded thoughtfully, switching the wipers on.

Well, there's two kinds of omens you know.

There are?

Of course. There's good ones and there's bad ones.

What kind is rain?

Rain is a good one, Dieter responded. Always has been.

Why?

Because rain makes things grow.

Like what?

Like corn. Like tomatoes.

The boy looked skeptical. You telling me if it didn't rain there wouldn't be any tomatoes?

That's exactly what I'm telling you!

They stopped outside a 7-11 so Hunter could call Toby. But when he returned to the truck he looked pensive. Toby, he reported, had overheard his mother tell his father that Hunter was in a place called *Limbo*. Where's Limbo, he asked his Mom.

Maggie considered her response before answering, camouflaging her anger at Lureen for saying such a thing. Limbo, she finally said, isn't a real place, it's a story place.

But where is it?

Maggie wasn't sure how to explain it. She looked over at Dieter for help.

He gave the boy a reassuring smile. Limbo, he said, is the place you stop at before you get to the place you wanna go.

Hunter thought about that for awhile before deciding that Limbo was a train station at dusk on the outskirts of a mountain village somewhere in the south of France. Men smoking big cigars stared out the depot's dark windows while their wives chatted with fellow travelers. The children squirmed on the station's hard benches, impatient for the train to whisk them away. Trains, depots, journeys. One night he dreamed about a black locomotive, shiny with ice, hurtling through a canyon. At the end of a corridor his father was lying in a pool of blood. He woke with a whimper, which woke his mother, too.

There now, she whispered, it was only a dream.

She slid into his bed and rubbed his bony shoulders until he fell back asleep. Then she lay in the dark listening to the swish of cars on the highway, wondering when, or more to the point if, the nightmares would end.

Dieter woke early and dressed in the dark. He bolted a cup of coffee in the lobby of the motel, then jogged across the highway to a small city park with a gravel path encircling the perimeter. An empty playground. Picnic tables. A chestnut tree. It felt good to be alone for awhile, to hike through the park in the cool morning air, to clear his mind of distractions. In a world of betrayal and mistrust the theme of his next book, he decided, would be forgiveness. How Dieter forgave Raul and Hunter forgave officer Kershaw and Maggie forgave the world for treating her the way it did. He paused in the shade of the chestnut tree and gazed across the highway and thought about the boy and his mother in their beds at the Holiday Inn. He was responsible for them now, just as they were responsible for him, and the book would be about that, too, the end of isolation. For if to be fully human was to embrace the suffering of those you love, he had come full circle, from grief to healing, from penance to prayer.

That afternoon, he swung off the main road and parked in the driveway of a modest country home. In the side yard there was a pair of sawhorses and a stack of lumber and an empty can of mahogany stain. He climbed out of the truck and leaned down and peeked through the open window at Hunter.

I'll be right back, 'kay?

'Kay.

Standing next to the pickup, Maggie noticed beyond the roofline of the house a wave of dark hills. In the spring, she thought, the beeches on the slope would wear jackets of new leaves and that's where the sun would rise, over their dark crowns, every morning.

Maggie? Dieter was crossing the lawn and there was an older

man with him now. The older man was wearing a faded denim shirt and a John Deere baseball cap.

Hunter stepped down from the truck to stand next to his mother. In the chill morning air he could see his own breath, like a wisp of cloud, dissolve into nothing.

Dieter was saying the boy's name but Hunter didn't hear him. He was trying to imagine what it felt like to be tethered to a spaceship by a slender cord. If you let go, your oxygen would eventually fail and you would glance back, for the final time, at the lost planet.

Hunter?

Finally the boy looked up. Dieter was standing in front of him, in the driveway, with an arm around the older man's shoulder.

Hunter, Maggie . . . I'd like you to meet my dad.

$\sim$

He sits at his old desk, writing. Outside it has begun to snow but his concentration is so pure, so complete, he doesn't even notice. Nor does he hear, in another part of the house, Maggie opening jars of tomatoes to make the marinara sauce, or his father helping the boy with lessons, long division today.

Eventually the winter light that spills through the window fades, and when Dieter finally puts down his pen he's astonished to discover that night has already fallen.

He opens a drawer, takes out his journal, and scribbles beneath the date: *three new pages, evening snow . . .*

About the Author

Tim Applegate was born in Ft. Benning, Georgia and grew up in Terre Haute, Indiana. In 1978 he obtained a B.A. in journalism and literature from Indiana University.

Tim has lived in Boston, Sarasota, Florida, and for the last twenty-two years on two acres in the foothills of the coastal range of western Oregon. For the last two decades he has owned and operated a commercial contracting business specializing in furniture and wood restoration for the hotel and cruise ship industries. In 2015 he retired from contracting to write full-time.

Tim is married and has two daughters. He grows wine grapes on his acreage, remains an avid hiker, and travels extensively.

Tim's poetry, essays, and short fiction have appeared in The Florida Review, The South Dakota Review, Lake Effect, and The Briar Cliff Review among many others. He is the author of the poetry collections *At the End of Day* (Traprock Books), *Drydock* (Blue Cubicle Press), and Blueprints (Turnstone Books of Oregon). *Fever Tree*, the first book of a projected trilogy, is his first published novel.